**'Sorry, but** ...
**following his** ...

Amy stated vehem... low profile out of the window. 'What is this, a dictatorship? The least he could do is discuss this with me before he starts changing things willy-nilly.'

Tess's face suddenly turned pink as she focused past Amy's shoulder. Amy instantly felt remorse for venting her anger on the receptionist. 'I apologise. I shouldn't be jumping all over you when I'd rather be jumping all over Dr Gregory.'

'An interesting proposition,' came the deep sexy drawl in her ear. 'Maybe we should discuss this somewhere more...*private*?'

Time seemed to stand still while Amy frantically tried to recover from the shock of Dr Gregory appearing unexpectedly and overhearing her remark. His emphasis on that one little word, uttered in just the right tone, sent an embarrassed heat spiralling upwards through her face.

# NURSES WHO DARE

**The Wyman sisters—**
**women who conquer their fears and emotions**
**and win the lives and loves they long for.**

In A NURSE'S FORGIVENESS Marta Wyman must
find it in her heart to forgive her grandfather for the act
that estranged him from her mother before Marta was
born. Dr Evan Gallagher is in New Hope to persuade
her to forgive and forget—especially as it becomes
clear that they can't be together until she does.

In A NURSE'S PATIENCE Amy loves her job
as a nurse-practitioner until Dr Ryan Gregory
joins the practice and questions her abilities.
She asks to work with another physician—
patience not being her strong point. But if she persists
she'll earn Ryan's trust and much, much more!

In A NURSE'S COURAGE Rachel Wyman
must find the courage to go back to the nursing
profession she loves after she is robbed of her
confidence when she is unable to help a dying friend.
Physician Nicholas Sheridan is the man to help her
rebuild her life. If she can find the courage
she'll not only win his trust, but his love.

**Look out for A NURSE'S COURAGE in 2002**

# A NURSE'S PATIENCE

BY
JESSICA MATTHEWS

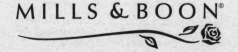

MILLS & BOON®

*All the characters in this book have no existence outside the imagination of the author, and have no relation whatsoever to anyone bearing the same name or names. They are not even distantly inspired by any individual known or unknown to the author, and all the incidents are pure invention.*

*First published in Great Britain 2001*
*Harlequin Mills & Boon Limited,*
*Eton House, 18-24 Paradise Road, Richmond, Surrey TW9 1SR*

© Jessica Matthews 2001

ISBN 0 263 82698 8

*Set in Times Roman 10½ on 11½ pt.*
*03-1101-49284*

*Printed and bound in Spain*
*by Litografia Rosés, S.A., Barcelona*

# CHAPTER ONE

SHE felt totally out of place.

Amy Wyman drew a deep breath and wiped her palms on her baggy trousers as she stood outside the clinic's conference room. At the moment, she was as noticeable as a peacock in a flock of sparrows.

It wasn't as if she didn't belong or have a right to be here. On the contrary, she should have arrived an hour ago for this auspicious occasion in the clinic's ten-year history. With the addition of two family practice physicians, Ryan Gregory and Joshua Jackson, to the line-up of obs and gynae staff, the Women's Clinic had become the Community Medical Clinic.

Up until now, women had comprised the medical group's patient population. By bringing doctors Gregory and Jackson on board, and a pediatrician within the next six months, the hope was for these women to also escort their husbands and children through the building's doors.

Dr Hyde's expansion plans also included a heart specialist, an oncologist and a dermatologist. Heaven only knew this southeast corner of Kansas had need of such skilled physicians, but the question many people asked was, Could they be lured here? The only golf course was carved out of a pasture and the cultural events consisted of a local jazz band and the high-school drama class. Only time would tell.

And speaking of time, the minutes were ticking away while she stood in the hallway gathering her courage to make what would surely be a grand, if not humorous entrance.

Although today's reception was in honor of both men, her supervising physician—Dr Jackson—had started nearly a month ago. If she missed his official welcoming bash, he wouldn't feel slighted.

On the other hand, Dr Hyde, the senior partner, had threatened dire consequences for anyone absent without a justifiable excuse, like a death certificate. As a new employee, she wasn't about to test him at his word. She might only have squeaked into the reception during the final fifteen minutes, but at least she'd put in an appearance.

If only the kids on Peds hadn't been especially clingy… If only little Cindy Chism hadn't been crying because her mother hadn't been able to visit her today… If only she'd been able to turn back the clock a half an hour so she could have made herself over in order to blend in with her colleagues.

A fairy godmother would have come in handy right about now.

Amy's carefully organized schedule had fallen apart at the seams. It had happened often enough during her career for her to have long since learned not to cry over it. Calming Cindy had taken precedence over a stuffy old meeting and she didn't regret having spent a single extra second on the pediatrics wing. If garnering extra attention was the price for bringing smiles to the children's faces, then so be it.

She drew a deep breath, adjusted her wig, then entered. To her relief, her friend and colleague, Pamela Scott, sat in the back row next to an empty chair. Amy slid into the seat, trying her best to be invisible, although she knew she had as much chance of that as she did of winning the lottery.

Pam, a forty-year-old divorcee who was currently trying to hook husband number three, leaned closer. "You're late."

"No kidding," Amy whispered.

"Nice outfit."

Amy grinned. "Thanks. Made it myself. Did I miss anything?"

Pam patted her hand and gave her a sympathetic glance. "Ignorance is bliss."

Intrigued by her friend's cryptic comment, but knowing further explanations would have to wait, Amy turned her attention to the front of the room. She recognized four of the clinic physicians, including Dr Hyde and Josh Jackson. By a process of elimination, the remaining guy at the head table had to be Dr Gregory.

In the next breath, she caught him studying her as closely as she was studying him. Considering her appearance, it was inevitable for her to attract his attention. However, she was also used to seeing a smile, a grin or even a laugh in return. Dr Gregory simply raised one dark eyebrow. The expression on his face didn't change; his full lips didn't twitch with any emotion resembling amusement as he pinned her under his watchful eye.

In the gaze that seemed to penetrate as deeply as a cardiac needle, she detected a distinct note of disapproval.

Too bad, she thought as she forced steel into her spine so as not to flinch under his disdainful scrutiny. She'd been on a mission of mercy. If the new doctor didn't like her late arrival or the way she looked, too bad. She didn't owe him any explanations.

Dr Hyde finished his comments and invited Dr Gregory to say a few words. As he rose, his height advantage over Dr Hyde became obvious. He had to be near the six-foot mark—at least a good eight inches more than she could claim.

His deep voice contained a hint of a southern drawl which she'd always considered remarkably sexy. His russet-colored hair was thick and curly and his features as well defined as if they'd been carved in granite. His smile as he greeted the audience softened the harshness to a large degree, but his grin seemed forced, as if he disliked being the center of attention.

Even if he hadn't been a guest of honor, he would have captured the notice of any woman who still had breath in her body. His suit fit his athletic form like a glove, and he moved with a loose-limbed grace that had to come from regular workouts. Idly, she wondered if he preferred sports or used exercise equipment. In any case, he didn't have a sedentary physique like so many of his colleagues. His female patients would probably exhibit elevated heart rates and high blood pressure once he walked through their exam-room doors.

What a shame he projected such a serious image, Amy decided as he glanced in her direction again. He was nice-looking, although a smile would make him devilishly handsome. The intensity of his piercing gaze seemed to raise the temperature in the room about ten degrees but she forced herself not to fidget.

Thank goodness she worked with Dr Jackson.

As aloof and distant as Dr Gregory appeared, she wondered what tales would spread through the grapevine concerning his bedside manner. He was probably one of those MDs who exhibited brilliance with diseases but was impaired in the people-skills department.

She sent up a silent prayer for his poor nurse, whoever she was. He clearly wasn't the type who would tolerate mistakes of any kind, much less unbend enough to develop a camaraderie with the staff. While Dr Jackson was easygoing to a fault, at least he didn't remind her of a hawk about to pounce on a hapless mouse.

She wondered if Dr Gregory's no-nonsense demeanor was typical of him or if he was simply nervous about being on display. He didn't appear uneasy or restless so she ruled out the latter theory. From the way he carefully looked over the small gathering, he was clearly sizing up everyone. In her case, he'd already found her wanting.

His loss, she decided. If he didn't want to relax, to kick up his heels and laugh along the treacherous road of life, then so be it. His attitude wasn't her problem.

Her only problem right now was the makeup running into her eyes. As soon as the formalities were over, she intended to head for her car—and home—as fast as her feet could carry her.

There was a first time for everything.

Ryan Gregory had attended meetings with people from all walks of life and had been wined and dined by a fair number of prestigious people during his medical career, but never had a bona fide *clown* dropped in during a formal staff meeting.

Never, that was, until today.

Seated with the other clinic doctors as they faced their audience, he watched with keen interest as the individual wearing oversized brown shoes managed to step lightly toward a vacant chair in the back row. The woman next to the clown smiled and whispered something, but otherwise didn't act as if this individual's presence—or attire—was unusual.

Which made the situation all the more intriguing.

Phillip Hyde, the senior partner in this clinic, had promised him a rousing welcome. Everything so far had been as expected—friendly faces, helpful people, punch and cookies. His imagination had certainly not stretched far enough to include comic relief.

While Phillip expounded at length on the changes the clinic would see in the months ahead, Ryan's attention wandered toward the person who stood out in this particular crowd of medical folk.

Between the rainbow-colored wig, the painted smile, white gloves and a baggy suit made of polka dots and stripes in mismatched, bold colors, he couldn't tell for certain if the latecomer was male or female. Size-wise, however, this particular clown possessed a fine facial bone structure and a petite frame which suggested the outlandish clothing and stage makeup disguised a woman.

He imagined the staff member seated in the audience to have the same anything-goes, out-for-a-good-time, fly-by-the-seat-of-one's-pants attitude as his former nurse-practitioner. Once he'd realized how she'd placed her hobbies and personal interests before her patients, he'd lost all confidence in her. In his opinion, that type of outlook didn't have a place in any job, much less the medical profession.

On a less serious note, the clown also reminded him of his mother. He loved her dearly but he could only describe her as a free spirit. She did what she wanted, *when* she wanted, without any concern for consequences. He'd learned to accept her impulsive style as being who she was, but he'd seen how her often outlandish actions had affected his more serious father. Conflicts had been many until they'd simply given up trying to reconcile their differences.

Dismissing the clown from his mind, he scanned the group before him in search of a woman with reddish-blonde hair. So far, no one had matched Phillip's description of his newly assigned nurse-practitioner. In a way, he was relieved she hadn't arrived. Tomorrow would be soon enough to meet her…and outline his expectations.

Supervising the elusive Ms Wyman wasn't a duty he wanted in any way, shape or form. Although he'd voiced his reservations and the reasons behind them, Phillip had insisted an NP was a necessity, not a luxury. "You'll thank me," the senior partner had said.

Ryan privately disagreed. The only thing he could thank him for was the additional work he'd be duty-bound to perform until he could trust the woman. Who knew how long, or if, that would ever happen? In theory, Phillip was right. An NP was an asset to a physician. By taking care of the straightforward cases, he or she freed the doctor for the more complicated ones. Or so he'd heard from a fair number of physicians who'd been more than satisfied with those in their employ.

Unfortunately, his experiences hadn't been as positive. One had been so unsure of herself that he'd ended up doing twice the workload. The other had been the complete opposite, and as a result had landed his practice in serious trouble. Ryan didn't want to live through a repeat of either of those scenarios.

Although he would have preferred interviewing and hiring an NP on his own terms, he was duty-bound to give the nurse-practitioner he'd inherited a trial period. He would...within reason. Over the next few weeks, he'd test her measure and give her only enough rope to tether her to his professional side. Any more than that carried with it the potential of hanging herself, and him as well. She would either prove her abilities or land in the unemployment line.

What a shame that his NP wasn't the no-nonsense fiftyish lady seated in the front row who was a throwback to an earlier generation of nurses who wore white uniforms and sensible white shoes.

''And now I believe Dr Gregory would like to say a few words,'' Phillip announced, settling back in his chair.

At the sound of his name, Ryan refocused his attention and flashed a small smile at the attentive audience. ''I'm excited to be in Maple Corners and to be a part of the clinic's expansion. I hope you'll be patient with me as I learn your routine and get to know each of you at the same time.''

His gaze landed on the clown before he gratefully returned the podium to Phillip.

Phillip rose. "As you can see, unlike myself, Dr Gregory isn't long-winded. Maybe I should ask him to chair all of our meetings."

"Hear! hear!" someone said in a voice that carried through the room.

Chuckles broke out and Phillip grinned. "Whoever said that has just volunteered to join the clean-up crew," he commented mildly.

In the middle row, a tall man wearing a pair of rimless glasses made a show of groaning. As his colleagues tittered and turned to tease him, he shrugged his shoulders good-naturedly.

Phillip turned to Ryan. "Are you ready to wind down and check out your suite of rooms?"

"Absolutely." Two hours of being in the limelight had been enough. He was more than ready to explore his work-place so he could start moving his books and other personal possessions.

Ryan followed Phillip around the table, conscious of the flamboyant individual who was still talking to the woman next to her. "By the way, who's the clown? You didn't plan any entertainment, I hope."

Phillip guffawed. "Sorry, old man. But I imagine you'll get to know her pretty well in the days ahead."

Ryan raised an eyebrow in question.

The clinic's senior partner slapped him between his shoulder blades. "You bet. Josh has been overseeing her for the past few weeks. Before that, she worked under George Garrett in his practice across town. He retired last month, so I snapped her up before someone else could."

"She's that good?"

Phillip nodded. "She moved to Maple Corners about six months ago, but I'd guess that she knows more people in town than those who've lived here for years. A professional marketing service won't bring you as many new patients as she will.''

''A real social butterfly,'' Ryan commented dryly. Even from this distance, he homed in on the sultry tones of her voice. His idea of a fun time was a quiet dinner and a movie while hers was probably dancing with every male in the building until dawn.

''Not as far as I know. She just has a way about her that attracts people. George couldn't sing her praises highly enough. According to him, she practically ran his office single-handedly. If you need anything, she'll either get it done or know the person who can.''

Thoughts of a highly efficient clerical person flashed through Ryan's mind. ''Good secretaries are hard to come by.''

Phillip guffawed. ''You'll find her better than a secretary. She's your nurse-practitioner.''

''I'm what?'' Amy stared at Pam in horror. It couldn't be. Someone had made a horrible mistake.

''You're going to work under Dr Gregory,'' Pam patiently repeated.

''There has to be some mix-up. You misunderstood.'' She'd worked with Dr Jackson for almost four weeks. Being assigned to another physician hadn't occurred to her.

Pam shook her head. ''I'm afraid not. Dr Jackson has both a nurse and you. Dr Gregory has neither so you've been chosen to help him.''

''It's only temporary, right?'' She crossed her fingers for luck.

''From the way Dr Hyde talked, it sounded permanent to me. But, hey, I could be wrong.''

Amy narrowed her eyes. ''If this is some sort of a joke…''

"Do I look like I'm laughing? Besides, you're the clown, not me."

Once again, Amy watched the man of the hour in his conversation with Dr Hyde. A few seconds later, a fleeting look of astonishment crossed his face before he raised one disapproving eyebrow at her.

Appearing late, and in her Sunshine-the-Clown suit, obviously hadn't given a positive first impression.

"He's turning purple," Amy commented. "He must have realized who I am." She turned her back so she wouldn't see his look of distaste and feel worse than she already did. She didn't need a degree in physics to know their working relationship would either blend like oil and water or be as explosive as dynamite.

For once, she'd proved Marta's advice wrong. It would have been better if she'd braved Dr Hyde's wrath in order to present herself in a more professional light. "I believe it's time for a hasty exit," she added under her breath.

"Do you think that's wise?" Pam asked. "I mean, you're here, and it'll look strange to everyone—especially to him—if you leave without introducing yourself."

"You didn't see the expression on his face. Take my word for it. He won't appreciate having a clown come up and say, 'Hi, I'm Amy and I'm looking forward to treating patients with you.' He doesn't seem the sort who would find it amusing."

"Come on. I've never seen you back down from anything before. Don't start now."

"I'm not backing down. I'm simply choosing my battleground."

"Well, you can't go now."

"And why not?"

"Because he's on his way over here," Pam muttered, plastering a huge smile on her face. "Hello, Dr Gregory. It's so nice to have you in our clinic."

He nodded. "Pam, isn't it?"

As her friend preened under his attention, Amy wished she could have met him under other circumstances—like tomorrow while she was wearing her scrubs and had the comfort of her stethoscope around her neck. It was tough to project a professional demeanor while wearing a clown suit, but she intended to do her best. Her friend, Sunny, who usually acted as Sunshine the Clown, owed her big time for asking her to fill in at the last minute.

"And, of course, this is Amy," Pam said, drawing the conversation around to her. "Won't you excuse me? There's someone I have to catch and I know you two have a lot to discuss."

Amy recognized Pam's attempt to leave them alone and glared at her friend before she disappeared into the crowd. Amy turned to Dr Gregory and extended one gloved hand. "It's a pleasure to meet you."

Ryan hesitated. "You're not booby-trapped, are you? No buzzer in your palm or anything else that might make offensive noises?"

His accusatory tone made her stiffen. He really must think she was a practical joker instead of someone who tried to take children's minds off their problems for a little while. This did not bode well for the success of their working relationship.

Holding up her hands she said curtly, "You're safe." He took her hand and the warmth she felt through her thin, white cotton glove instantly unsettled her.

"For a doctor, you have warm hands." The words slipped out of her mouth before she could stop them. As a clown, she'd said outlandish things to make people smile. Unfortunately, she needed to impress him with her professional persona and not her stage act.

"Thank you. I think."

Amy's nerve endings tingled until, in the space of a heartbeat, the sparks coalesced into an electrical current running up her arm. Surprised by the reaction generated in just a few short seconds, she inhaled sharply and breathed in a blend of sandalwood, coffee and something indescribably male.

Oh, dear. She was in trouble if she found his scent…sexy. Why couldn't a nauseating odor surround him? But, no, he had to smell good enough to kick a woman's hormones into overdrive.

Amy released his hand, conscious of how he towered over her and made her seem shorter than usual. If she'd learned one thing in her twenty-seven years of living, she'd seen how a fair number of people assumed intelligence was proportional to height. She couldn't afford to be at such a disadvantage with her new boss.

On the other hand, if anyone needed to loosen up a bit, it was Ryan Gregory. An imp of mischief urged her on. Surely she could draw a smile out of him somehow. Her reputation as a clown—albeit a temporary one—was at stake.

Dressed as she was, she felt she could ask questions she normally wouldn't have dreamed of asking, and say things she normally wouldn't have dreamed of saying. "You don't laugh often, do you, Dr Gregory?"

He shrugged, but the heat in his smoke-colored eyes suggested that he was far from nonchalant. "When the occasion calls for it."

"Then you're always this serious?"

"Are you always this nosy with your colleagues?" he countered.

"Right now, we're not colleagues," she reminded him. "I'm a clown, remember?"

"I'm not likely to forget. So how often does your alter ego surface?"

"Not very often. I fill in for a friend of mine whenever she can't make it. She visits the hospital every week and spends most of her time on Pediatrics."

"I see." He seemed to mull over her answer. "What tricks do you do?"

"It's easier to show than to tell." Amy dug in her left pocket and flourished a long, narrow black rod. Silk flowers instantly bloomed from one end.

"Nice," he said, his voice even.

Her clown side demanded more of a response than an insipid "nice." She handed the rod to him and watched him take it gingerly.

"It won't blow up, you know."

"Thanks for the reassurance."

"The kids always like the hanky trick." Out of another pocket, she pulled a yellow square of cloth which was tied to a blue square, then to a red square, until finally a small pile of fabric pooled at her feet. Then she untied the last piece and pantomimed blowing her nose before she made a fist and poked it inside with her index finger. In a wink, she opened her fingers to reveal an empty palm.

Ordinarily, children oohed and aahed, while adults watched with amazement on their faces. Dr Gregory didn't crack a smile, although she thought a spark of interest glimmered in his eyes.

"Cute," he said.

She didn't know if "cute" was a step above or below "nice" and decided not to ask.

"When do you pull the rabbit out of a hat?"

"I'm a clown, not a magician," she said tartly. "But if you want an animal to appear, I'll do my best." She dug deeply into another pocket of her voluminous trousers and removed a twelve-inch purple balloon about the same diameter as her little finger.

She began blowing. Several squeaky twists and turns later, she presented him with a poodle. "How's that?"

Ryan studied it for a few seconds, then placed it on the chair. "Pretty good, but poodles are rather standard balloon animals, aren't they?"

She ground her teeth. Nothing made a clown see red faster than a person who acted bored during a performance, and her vision was starting to cloud. "I suppose you can do better?"

This time, the corners of his mouth turned up slightly. As a smile, it lacked wholeheartedness, but since his eyes seemed to sparkle, she was willing to call it one.

"Is that a challenge?" he asked.

"Yes," she dared. "I'm always looking for something new to add to my repertoire."

He reached out to touch her left ear. For a second, she couldn't breathe from anticipation, but his touch was light as he tugged on her earlobe. She had this strange urge to rub her cheek along his sleeve, then press his palm to her face.

Ryan pulled his arm back to display a quarter pinched between his thumb and index finger. "How's this?"

She was amazed at his sleight of hand. She hadn't mastered the technique of pulling coins out of obscure places and she'd been working on it for a long time. "I'm impressed."

He flipped the coin, caught it in midair, then sandwiched her right hand between both of his as he pressed the money into her palm.

"What's this for?" she asked.

"Your tip."

Amy drew back her hand as if scalded. "Sorry, but I don't take tips. It's against my policy."

"Fine," he said. "Then may I offer a verbal one instead?"

She waited expectantly for him to continue.

"No one pulls the wool over my eyes," he said smoothly. "Keep that in mind and we'll get along just fine."

# CHAPTER TWO

AMY froze, her mental alarms screaming as she read between the lines of Ryan Gregory's statement. He might have spoken softly, but his tone didn't disguise the underlying steel. After sensing his instant dislike during the presentation, the implications behind his comment were obvious. He wasn't referring to clown tricks, but to her professional habits and abilities. His admonition grated on her nerves and filled her with indignation.

His whole attitude reminded her of one long-ago professor who hadn't been able to see any shades of gray and who'd followed the rules without allowing any margin for error, mercy or second chances. Dr Gregory clearly fitted the same personality mold.

She placed her hands on her hips and glared at him. The flower on her hat danced in front of her eyes and she swatted it away as if it were a pesky fly.

Too bad she couldn't do the same to Dr Gregory.

"And just what are you implying?" she demanded. "That I'm incompetent? That I'm not open and honest in my dealings? What?"

"I'm not hinting at anything. I was stating a fact."

Huh, she inwardly scoffed. She recognized a warning when she heard one. "Why don't you just say exactly what you mean?"

He hesitated. "I haven't been particularly satisfied with my last two nurse-practitioners."

"So you're assuming you'll be just as disappointed with me," she accused.

"I'm not assuming anything," he insisted. "Which is

19

why I intend to keep a close eye on your work until we get to know each other.''

"Until you decide I'm capable," she corrected.

He shrugged. ''I prefer to look at the next several months as a time of learning each other's strengths and weaknesses.''

Amy had a sneaking suspicion he was more interested in her weaknesses than strengths. ''You look at a glass as half-empty rather than half-full, don't you?''

His eyebrows drew together slightly. ''I beg your pardon?''

"Never mind. But, for the record, I've not had anyone complain about my work before.''

He crossed his arms. ''Then we shouldn't have any problems, should we, Ms Wyman?''

His condescending tone infuriated her. ''No, we shouldn't,'' she said through gritted teeth.

"I see you two have found each other.'' Phillip Hyde joined them, clearly oblivious to the charged atmosphere. ''Getting acquainted?''

"Yes, we are,'' Ryan said evenly.

"I knew you two would get along fine,'' Phillip crowed. ''I hate to interrupt but a reporter from the *Maple Corners News* wants to talk to you, Ryan. Can you spare him a few minutes?''

Amy stepped backward. ''Don't keep him waiting on my account. We've said everything that needs to be said at this point. Wouldn't you agree, Dr Gregory?''

"More or less, but I'm looking forward to continuing our discussion.''

She forced a smile but didn't reply.

As the two men headed in the opposite direction, Joshua Jackson caught her before she reached the door.

"I'm sorry to lose you,'' he said. ''When I suggested to

Dr Hyde to find someone like my NP to orient Dr Gregory, I never dreamed he'd steal you out from under my nose.''

She smiled. Dr Jackson had a face that only a mother—or his wife—would have loved, including a nose that was rather large for his thin face.

"Maybe you could tell him you exaggerated,'' she suggested brightly.

"I tried," he mourned, "but he didn't buy my story. Still, you'll like Ryan. He was an intern when I started medical school, you know.''

She hadn't, but that was beside the point.

"He's quiet but, I swear, he doesn't miss a thing.''

"Great,'' she said weakly. His private comment to her now sounded more like a promise than a mere threat.

Josh patted her arm. "Don't worry.''

*Don't worry,* she told herself as she fled from the building. Eager didn't begin to describe how she felt about leaving, and this time no one would stop her. She had too much to think about. Her plum job had suddenly become something of a nightmare.

*He doesn't miss a thing.*

The thought sent an unreasonable wave of panic through her. Medically, she played it strictly by the book. Taking care of her patients was first and foremost in her mind and she wouldn't risk their health. It was just that sometimes she stretched the rules a bit. She made an occasional house call and conveniently ''forgot'' to bill a patient for services rendered if they couldn't afford it. People like the Mullens came to mind. They struggled with more problems than most and had recently added their son's diabetic condition to the list.

She sincerely doubted whether Dr Gregory would be as forgiving or as supportive of her generosity as Dr Garrett had been. Dr Jackson, of course, hadn't known her long enough to catch her performing what she considered as missions of mercy.

"Wait up!" Pam's familiar voice reverberated across the parking lot.

Amy unlocked the car door and slid inside. Her only concession to her friend was to lower the window. "You called?" she asked.

"How did it go?" Pam demanded.

"Interesting," she said curtly, unwilling to say more until she'd sorted through her conversation with her new boss at length. "We met and now I'm going home."

Pam rolled her eyes. "Come on. I want details. What did you think of Dr Gregory?"

"It's too soon to make a decision."

"Well, then, what was your first impression? He seems like the strong, silent type." She sighed. "I do love a man of few words. Reminds me of Cary Grant. Now, *he* was a man I'd take home without thinking twice." She finished with a wink.

"Then why don't *you* work for him and *I'll* work for Dr Brooks."

A worried furrow appeared between Pam's eyebrows. "That bad already?"

Amy clutched the steering-wheel and stared straight ahead to avoid her friend's gaze. "It depends on how you define 'bad'. Apparently my degree and experience don't mean a thing in his eyes. I could have gotten my diploma out of a cereal box."

"Aren't you overreacting a bit?"

Amy met Pam's gaze. "I don't think so. According to him, he's going to keep a close eye on me."

"He doesn't know you, so it's understandable."

Amy sighed at her friend's practicality. "I suppose, but how would you feel if Dr Brooks watched every move you made?"

"He does," Pam said smugly. "If things don't fly with my computer consultant, I may say yes the next time he asks for a date."

"You know what I mean."

"It won't be as bad as you think," Pam consoled.

"Oh, yeah? You should have heard the *way* he delivered his little piece of advice. He was warning me to toe the line, plain and simple. Not only that, but he said he'd be watching me for *months*." Her stomach dropped to her toes at the thought.

Pam smiled. "You know what your problem is, Amy?"

"I'm sure you're about to tell me," she said dryly.

"You're too used to doing your own thing. Let's face it. Dr Garrett was so close to retirement he didn't care what you did or didn't do. And Dr Jackson can hardly handle the load he has, much less worry about yours."

While Pam's observation rang true, there was one important difference. "They *trusted* me," Amy said. "Which is more than Dr Gregory is willing to do."

"He will," Pam predicted. "Give him time."

"Until that magic moment arrives, he's going to make my life miserable. And speaking of feeling miserable..." she adjusted her wig because her scalp had begun to itch "...I've got to get out of this costume before I melt." July days were notoriously warm and, thanks to air-conditioning, she normally didn't find her costume too uncomfortable. However, that didn't apply when sitting in a sunbaked vehicle.

Pam patted her shoulder and gave her a reassuring smile. "Yeah, your face is dripping."

"Gee thanks."

"Any time. Meanwhile, don't worry about ole Doc Gregory. Once his schedule fills up, he won't give you a second thought."

Amy's spirits lifted. "You're right. I've already seen his

first week's appointment book. He'll be busy from morning until night.''

"See?" Pam leaned closer. "After having been married twice, I've learned a lot about the male psyche. A sure way to get what you want is to let them think it's their idea.''

"Do you think so?" Amy asked. His wool-over-the-eyes comment suggested that he was well aware of any and all tactics one might use.

"Believe me. It'll work every time," Pam declared. "Play along for a few days if that's what it takes to make him happy. By next Friday, you'll have proven how capable you are and will be on your own again.''

At home, Amy repeated those thoughts like a mantra while she transformed herself from Sunshine the Clown to Amy, regular person. Pam's theory had to be right. Patience not being her strong suit, she couldn't stand the idea of working under a man who tied her professional hands at every turn.

Her only other choice was to go elsewhere, but quitting wasn't a viable option. She had too much to prove to her ex-boyfriend, her sisters and herself to start over again. Following her principles and championing the underdogs hadn't helped her build a fabulous résumé. Besides, it had taken her six months to find a job she liked in a town she enjoyed and she wasn't willing to sever the ties she'd already made.

Pam's theory simply *had* to be right.

And just to make sure, she intended to stack the odds in her favor. After taking her cocker spaniel, Mindy, for her daily run and forgoing a dip in her neighbor's pool, she spent her evening reviewing the policies and protocols that Dr Jackson had already approved. Her success over the next few days depended on not doing a single, solitary thing that might give Dr Gregory grounds to complain about her. She would dazzle him with her brilliance and efficiency.

On Tuesday, Amy took great pains with her appearance. She wore a teal blue scrubsuit with a multicolored teddy-bear smock top, used a light touch with her makeup since anything more made her appear like a little girl playing dress-up, and pinned her hair in the tight bun she usually wore in the office.

Let Dr Gregory find fault with her today, she mentally dared.

She arrived at the clinic at her usual time—thirty minutes before her first scheduled patient. As she walked along the right leg of the U-shaped corridor to her office, she took pride in her wing of the building. It had been part of the latest renovation and the decor was bright and cheery.

She particularly liked the floor plan. The three sections of the corridor circled a common area where the patients waited and where the receptionist worked. The upper half of the wall separating the two was glass, causing the staff to affectionately refer to this portion of the office as the ''goldfish bowl''. Doors on either side granted patient access to whichever rooms were available.

Medical records were stored near the rear of the receptionist's domain although the most distant section had been partitioned off for Amy's desk. A nearby door allowed her to slip in and out of her office from the exam cubicles without bothering the receptionist or being seen by those waiting.

What she took greatest satisfaction from, however, was the nurse's room. She'd transferred the medications from the tiny closet in the left corner to the exam room in the dead center of the U and filled it with all sorts of supplies that were necessary but not needed in each cubicle.

Because she handled her own nursing duties of drawing blood, administering injections and performing a wide array of other tasks, she liked having the more spacious quarters.

Staff in the other wings had been green with envy once they had seen her creation.

With any luck, Dr Gregory would appreciate her efforts as well. Of course, she wouldn't see his reaction for some time because his office hours started later than hers. Most physicians visited their hospital patients before coming to the clinic, so her day would be well under way before he walked through the door.

She couldn't have been more wrong.

"What do you mean, I've been moved?" Amy asked Tess, the receptionist who had just caught her as she rounded the corner.

The thirty-five-year-old brunette appeared more harried than usual at eight o'clock. She normally didn't get that look on her face until at least nine when the clinic opened and the phone calls started pouring in from patients who'd become ill overnight and wanted an immediate appointment.

"You're not really moved," she explained. "You're just sort of, well, *condensed*."

"Condensed?" Amy repeated, feeling as if she'd been relegated to the status of a can of soup. "What is *that* supposed to mean?"

"It means you have to share this wing with Dr Gregory."

Working under Dr Jackson had spoiled her. His office area had been small, so she'd moved into the suite next door. She'd been a hop and a skip away if she needed his opinion, yet isolated enough to maintain her feeling of independence.

She'd hoped to have the same sort of arrangement with Dr Gregory. Apparently, that had been wishful thinking. His comment about learning her strengths and weaknesses took on new meaning. Working in the same hallway, he would be in a position to literally watch her every move.

What a scary—and disheartening—thought.

"I'm sure I can live with half as much space," Amy said, struggling to think positive. "I have two sisters. I learned how to share."

The strange expression on Tess's face warned Amy of more bad news to come. "I do get half, don't I?"

Tess appeared uncomfortable. "Not exactly. The three rooms on the left will be yours."

"Three?" Amy asked, feeling her blood pressure rise. Although she'd had access to the eight cubicles—nine if she counted her nurse's room—along the U-shaped corridor, she'd never used them all. However, on extremely busy days, she'd managed to fill five. Granted, those occasions had been rare, but knowing the cubicles had been available had been nice. Apparently, he planned to see the lion's share of their patients.

Tess nodded, her face a picture of worry.

"All right, then," Amy said with an equanimity she didn't feel. She had a sneaky suspicion that the key to getting along with Dr Gregory was to maintain as low a profile as possible. "Let's get started."

Just then, Harry and Eldon, the two men who were responsible for most of the maintenance on the building, sauntered down the hall. Harry, a portly middle-aged man, waved at her while Eldon, a shy fellow in his early twenties, simply grinned.

"Hello, lovely ladies," he said with a smile. "We're here to move the refrigerator and two cabinets. Where do you want them?"

"Refrigerator?" Amy asked, puzzled by their request. They only had one and she wanted it right where it was—in the special quarters she'd created. As for the cabinets, she couldn't get by without them.

Tess pointed to Amy's pride and joy. "They're in

Number Five. Please move them to the old med. room at the end of the hall.''

Harry scratched his graying head. ''I don't think everything will fit.''

''What doesn't fit will have to go into storage,'' Tess instructed.

''Fair enough.'' Harry followed Eldon who was pushing the two-wheeled dolly they would use to move the heavy items.

Amy turned to Tess. ''The closet at the end?'' she said. ''You need a shoe spoon to squeeze two people in there. What's happening to my nurse's room?''

Tess shrugged. ''Dr Gregory is turning it into his office.''

''His office? What about all the equipment? The supplies, the centrifuge?''

''Talk to him. He said something about it being more efficient to stock supplies in every cubicle instead of just one.''

''There isn't *space* to do that,'' Amy argued. ''The drawers and cupboards are already full. What am I supposed to do with the things we need but rarely use?''

Tess held up her hands. ''Hey, I'm not the one making the decisions around here. I only do what I'm told and I was told to arrange for the guys to move those three pieces.''

''Sorry, but I'm not blindly following his orders,'' Amy stated vehemently, tossing her plan of a low profile out the window. ''What is this, a dictatorship? The least he could do is discuss this with me before he starts throwing his weight around and changing things willy-nilly.''

Tess's face suddenly turned pink as she focused past Amy's shoulder. Amy instantly felt remorse for venting her anger on the hapless woman. ''I apologize. I shouldn't be jumping all over you, when I'd rather be jumping all over Dr Gregory.''

"An interesting proposition," came the deep sexy drawl in her ear. "Maybe we should discuss this somewhere more…*private*?"

Tess made a small choking sound while Amy froze. For her, time seemed to stand still while she frantically tried to recover from the shock of Dr Gregory appearing unexpectedly and overhearing her remark. His emphasis on that one little word, uttered in just that tone, sent an embarrassed heat spiraling upward through her face.

Although she knew beyond all doubt, she had to ask. "He's behind me, isn't he?"

Tess nodded, her smile apologetic. "I'll check on Harry and Eldon," she squeaked, before she fled in the opposite direction.

It was time to face the dragon. Instead of dazzling him with her professionalism, she'd sounded like a whiny schoolchild. Amy drew a deep breath, then pivoted to greet her new boss.

If the masculine appreciation she saw on his face for a fleeting moment was any indication, she hadn't totally failed in the first-impression department. He was plainly surprised by what her clown makeup had disguised.

In the next instant, he frowned. "Are you sure you're twenty-seven?"

Appearing younger than her age was a fact she'd rued since she'd reached sixteen. Being short of stature, she couldn't begin to count the number of times she'd been mistaken for a twelve-year-old. Although she knew she'd appreciate those youthful genes when she reached her forties, at the moment resembling an eighteen-year-old was a definite drawback.

"According to my birth certificate, I am."

His face settled back into the formidable lines she'd observed yesterday. Although he was dressed more casually in an open-necked shirt and trousers, he still managed to exude an aura of authority and cool detachment that none of the other doctors could quite match.

Once again, his rock-solid equilibrium was in place and she wondered what it would take to ruffle his composure. Because she desperately wanted this job, antagonizing the boss wasn't the way to go about keeping it.

Pam's advice echoed in her mind. *Play along for a few days.*

Playing along didn't mean rolling over and acting dead, her independent self argued.

*To get what you want, make them think it's their idea.*

Amy stiffened her resolve. She could do this. Before she could form a sentence, he spoke.

"You mentioned a dictatorship?"

She drew a deep breath and tried to sound calm. "Since this change affects me as well as you, it would have been nice to discuss moving my med. room beforehand."

"I'd planned to, but you didn't work yesterday and then left rather suddenly after the reception."

"I'd asked to have the day off," she said defensively. Sunny had needed an emergency root canal and because Amy's schedule had been light, she'd rearranged her appointments so the children in the hospital wouldn't be disappointed. If she'd known about her reassignment, she would have made other plans.

Ryan shrugged. "I didn't think you'd mind where I put my office."

Mind? Of course she minded. She wanted him at the far end of their wing. Transforming cubicle five into a nurse's room might have been an impulsive move, but she'd proved its worth. In one fell swoop, he'd ruined everything.

As if realizing he needed to smooth over the newly troubled waters, he gave her a smile that fell short of being sincerely apologetic. "Nurses always complain about being on their feet all day. I assumed you'd appreciate saving a few steps.''

The new location *would* shorten her walking distance now that she'd been relegated to one hall, but the exercise was a fair trade for more spacious quarters.

She was all set to tell him so when her little voice interrupted. *Play along.*

Amy struggled to speak evenly while hoping she wouldn't get struck by lightning during the next storm for her white lie. ''I'm flattered by your gesture, but I'm a little concerned where we'll store everything. Our exam rooms don't have a lot of cupboard or drawer space.''

''I'm sure you'll make it work,'' he said mildly. ''If you have any suggestions, I'll certainly consider them.''

The only suggestion hovering on her lips wasn't appropriate and would probably get her fired.

She bit back the comment and offered another in an offhand manner. ''I'm surprised you wanted your private office in the middle of a busy hallway. You won't have much peace and quiet.''

He shrugged. ''I like to be where the action is.''

*All the better to see you, my dear, said the wolf to Little Red Riding Hood.* The line from the children's story seemed custom-made for her situation.

''By the way, I'm not territorial,'' he added calmly, as if unaware of her disappointment to steer him into reconsidering his decision. ''If you need more than three rooms, feel free to use mine if one's available.''

She could hardly mutter her grudging thanks before he continued. ''We're working *together*, not against each other. Our patients should see us as two resources in managing their health care.''

If she'd heard this speech before his don't-pull-the-wool-over-my-eyes warning yesterday, she would have counted her blessings for working with a doctor who possessed such an open-minded attitude. However, she hadn't, and now she considered his yours-mine-and-ours statement suspect.

"With you watching every move I make."

"Trust is earned."

"I've earned my diploma," she stated.

"But I'm the one with the medical degree," he reminded her. "I have a moral and a legal responsibility to oversee our patients' care."

Her jaw was starting to ache from the tension of holding back. Clearly, she wouldn't change his mind with mere words. If he wanted to review every sore throat and earache that came her way and wore himself out in the process, he wouldn't garner any sympathy from her.

*Play along.* Amy drew a tremulous breath. For the time being, retreat seemed in her best interests. "Suit yourself."

"Being transferred to my practice was a surprise for you, I know, but do you have a problem with temporarily acting as my nurse along with your other duties?"

"I'll get by," she ground out.

"Good. If you can recommend any nurses for our position, you might send them my way."

She started to tell him to check with the clinic's personnel department, then held her tongue. He'd asked for her opinion and she wasn't about to ruin this opportunity to find a suitable candidate. This might be her only chance for input. If she wasn't careful, he'd select someone like Betty Jean Post who had absolutely no sense of humor and was as much fun to be around as a corpse. She quickly ran through a list of potential RNs in her mind.

"Dora Wells might be interested." At his enquiring glance, she added, "She's in her forties and, if I remember correctly, her oldest is leaving the nest for college this fall. She may want full-time hours."

"Dora Wells," he repeated. "OK. Anyone else?"

"She's the only one who comes to mind. I'll put the word out, though."

"All right." For a few seconds, neither spoke. Only the bumping and scraping of furniture and Harry's sharp curses floated through the air. As the two men carted one of her cabinets off to the basement, Amy clenched her fists. She normally thought of herself as an easygoing person who could get along with just about anyone, but Dr Gregory was bringing out the worst in her.

Feeling as if they had said everything that needed to be said, she turned away to lick her wounds in private.

Before she took one step, he stopped her. "I'm not the enemy, Amy."

Raising her chin as she stared at him, she said quietly, "That remains to be seen, Dr Gregory."

He pursed his lips and gave a brief nod as if to acknowledge the challenge.

Walking with a dignity that contradicted the turmoil in her emotions, she headed for her desk and wished for real walls to hide behind rather than movable partitions. She sank onto her chair and pinched the bridge of her nose.

"What's wrong?" Tess peered over the chest-high barrier. "Headache?"

"Not yet, but I predict one is coming."

"Did you get everything ironed out with Dr Gregory?"

"If you're referring to my nurse's room then, no, we didn't. For everything else…? We're making progress."

Relief flooded across Tess's face. "I'm glad. I'm not eager to walk into a war zone every day."

"I'm not either, but be prepared," Amy warned. "The time for fireworks hasn't passed yet."

Tess sighed. "I hope you're not expecting me to referee."

Amy smiled. "Maybe once in a while." She grew serious. "It would be so much easier if I could make sense out of the things he does. The man is an enigma."

"What do you mean?"

Amy tried to organize her thoughts in a way she could explain. "He comes across as so serious, so decisive, so *controlling*. Then, out of the blue, he'll say something really profound about how we're partners. He even asked for suggestions on who to hire as our nurse. I can't tell which guy is the real Dr Gregory."

Tess shrugged. "Remember how awful our teachers seemed on the first day of school? They had to sound tough in order to put the fear of God in us. Then, by the end of the semester, they relaxed and we thought they were decent human beings."

"Yes, but some acted like jerks all year long," Amy reminded her. "Which category does Dr Gregory fit into?"

"You'll have plenty of opportunity to decide," Tess said dryly as she passed a folder to her. "In the meantime, you can sort out Blythe Anderson."

"I guess this means our day has officially begun."

Tess gave her a sympathetic glance, as if she, too, had reservations about having Dr Gregory underfoot at all times. "Good luck."

Amy managed a weak smile. "Thanks. I think we'll both need it."

# CHAPTER THREE

AMY greeted Blythe with a cheery good morning. "How's the wrist doing?"

The slightly overweight, salt-and-pepper-haired woman held out her right hand encased in a wrist support wrap, and flexed her fingers. "Coming along nicely. It hardly hurts any more."

Amy quickly took her temperature with the ear thermometer. "Rest and an anti-inflammatory does wonders."

"Yes, but who would have thought I would get tendinitis from hoeing my garden." Blythe shook her head. "I've planted and weeded and watered for nearly my whole life and never had a single problem."

Amy placed a blood pressure cuff around Blythe's arm and began pumping. "I hate to say it, but as we get older we have to expect some wear and tear to show once in a while."

Blythe grinned. "I know. I just hate to think of not being able to do everything I'd like. Inside this fifty-year-old body is the soul of a twenty-five-year-old."

Amy laughed. "You're lucky. Some days I feel like I should be ready to retire." She stuck the stethoscope tips in her ears and began listening. As soon as she'd noted the reading, she unfurled the screw and the final gasp of air left the cuff in a slow whoosh. "What can I do for you?"

Blythe grew serious. "I've got my urine infection again. This weekend, I started feeling the usual symptoms of back pain, et cetera." She waved her hand in an all-encompassing motion. "I started on my home remedy of cranberry juice and gave myself until today for it to work."

"It obviously hasn't."

She shook her head. "No. I guess it's time to see the specialist you told me about."

"Afraid so. Before we get carried away with plans, though, let's test a urine sample." Amy opened a cupboard and removed a sterile specimen cup and cleansing wipes. "You know the routine."

"I wish I didn't," Blythe grumbled good-naturedly.

While she disappeared down the hallway to the bathroom, Amy went in search of her next patient.

Tess handed her several folders. "These people want to see Dr Gregory."

Amy glanced at the names recorded on each tab. The last names were the same. "A family?"

Tess nodded. "Just moved to town. They're shopping for a physician."

"Fair enough." Amy called for the Inman family. A well-dressed young mother, carrying a two-year-old boy with his thumb in his mouth, and a five-year-old girl responded and she ushered them to one of Dr Gregory's rooms.

"I'm Lucinda Inman," the woman informed her haughtily. The diamond on her left hand was the size of Gibraltar and her brown hair had obviously been done by a stylist. Her pale blue shorts and matching sleeveless shirt obviously fell in the designer label category and had been chosen to show off her tanned skin and the sculpted muscles she'd earned from gym workouts.

"And these two are Tyler and Theresa," Mrs Inman went on. Both children were equally well dressed. The toddler wore a navy and red sailor suit and the little girl wore a yellow sun dress. Both had light hair and clung to their mother as if they were afraid of this experience.

Amy smiled at them both. "Hello, Tyler and Theresa. Have you gone swimming this summer?"

Tyler didn't remove his thumb but his big brown-eyed gaze followed her movements. Theresa nodded.

"We've just moved to town from Topeka," Lucinda said. "And we want to locate a physician."

"You've come to the right place," Amy remarked, winking at the little girl who stood behind her mother's chair as if to make herself invisible. At Theresa's bashful smile, Amy opened the top folder to scan the patient questionnaire.

"Any significant medical history?" she asked.

"We're a healthy family," Lucinda reported a trifle smugly. "We exercise, eat right and take vitamins."

"And the children?"

"The usual childhood things…colds, earaches, sore throats. Theresa had an appendectomy last January, but otherwise none of us have been in the hospital."

Amy closed the folder and quickly scanned the next two. Nothing remarkable jumped out at her, although Lucinda had marked a history of heart disease and lung cancer in the maternal side of the family. She circled those in red to draw Dr Gregory's attention to them.

"Everything looks in order," she said.

Theresa piped up. "Are you the doctor?" she asked.

Amy smiled. "No, I'm a nurse-practitioner." At her puzzled frown, she clarified. "I get to do some of the things a doctor does, but not all of them. If you get an earache or if your throat hurts, I can give you medicine, but if you have a sore tummy like you did when you went to the hospital, then a doctor will take care of you."

"Oh. Do you give shots?"

Amy laughed as Theresa edged herself farther behind Lucinda's chair. "Yes, I do, but you're not sick today, are you?"

Theresa shook her head so that her short curls bounced.

"I don't give shots to kids who aren't sick," Amy reassured her.

"Does the doctor give shots if we're not sick?"

"Absolutely not."

Theresa's face showed her express relief and she edged back to her spot beside her mother.

Amy grinned. "I'll send the doctor in so you can talk." She slipped the folders in the slot outside the door.

A quick check showed that Blythe hadn't returned to her room, so she went to call the next patient. She recognized her real estate agent, Dean Woods, so she showed him to one of her cubicles.

"No need to ask what your problem is," she teased, noting his red swollen left eye as she tugged on latex gloves. A closer glance revealed crusted matter on the lid.

Dean sat on the exam table. "It's quite a sight, isn't it?"

"What happened?"

"I was using my edge-trimmer last night," Dean confessed. "Normally, I wear goggles, but I only had a little section to trim, so I didn't. Before I knew it, there was a cloud of dust and I felt grass and dirt hit my face."

"Did you rinse your eyes right away?" she asked.

"Yeah. My wife used some solution she keeps on hand. They felt better, but as the evening went on I could have sworn that I still had sand in the one."

Amy stripped the gloves off her hands. Considering how his problem had come about, she was reasonably certain his infection was bacterial. "I'm going to irrigate your eye again, just to be sure we've removed all the foreign particles. Then I'll prescribe some antibiotic drops. Your eye should be back to normal in a few days." She wondered if the clinic had a slit lamp to check for corneal abrasions. The obs and gynae department probably wouldn't have one, so she made a mental note to call Dr Jackson's nurse and ask.

"Good. I had to cancel an important meeting at the bank today. I didn't think it would look too professional to show up with a weepy eye."

"Probably not. I'll fetch my supplies and be back in a few minutes."

On the way, she retrieved Blythe's urine sample and hurried into the nurse's room, not realizing her wrong turn until she'd crossed the threshold. A massive walnut desk which hadn't been there earlier occupied most of the space and Ryan Gregory was seated behind it.

He looked up from the papers in his hand and raised one questioning eyebrow.

"Excuse me," she muttered, "I forgot this isn't my…my room any more. Sorry."

One corner of his mouth lifted. "No problem. Drop by any time."

"There's a family here to see you," she said.

He glided away from his desk on quiet wheels before he rose. "I'll be right there."

Amy backtracked to the med. room which had been restored to service, grumbling at the limited space. Luckily, Harry and Eldon had squeezed the cabinet containing her main supplies between the door and the wall. Thankful that she didn't have to play hunt the bottle for her reagent strips, she dipped Blythe's sample and waited the required two minutes to read the results.

The small patches indicating the presence of bacteria and white cells turned pink, which meant positive. Blythe definitely had another urinary tract infection.

Amy washed her hands, wondering where her stock of normal saline had ended up as that particular cabinet was missing. She'd look for it just as soon as she'd dealt with Blythe.

She charged into the woman's room and stopped short.

"Dr Gregory," she said, wondering if he was aware that this was her patient.

He turned toward her, looking very professional in his white coat. "Blythe was just telling me about her history. Do you have her urine results?"

Amy fought her anger at his intrusion. She hadn't had a physician drop in without her express request since her NP training. "Positive for protein, white cells and bacteria."

He glanced at the older woman. "I agree with Amy's assessment. An appointment with a urologist is definitely in order."

Amy should have felt relief that he concurred with her decision, but she didn't. She'd had no idea that his "keeping an eye on her" would be so blatant.

"What do you think is wrong?" Blythe asked.

"It could be a number of things," he admitted. "The most obvious is that women of your age lose their muscle tone and don't always empty the bladder completely. Eventually, an infection develops. Regardless, the urologist will be able to give you more answers after he sees you."

He glanced at Amy. "What antibiotic were you going to use?"

"Since this is her third episode, I thought to use sulfa and trimethoprim," she said stiffly.

"Good choice. It appears you've been in excellent hands, Blythe. It was nice to meet you." His smile to the woman was full of sincerity, which shocked Amy no end. If only he would smile like that around her, she thought. It would go a long way to making her feel like a valued colleague and not a toddler who had to be watched every second of the day.

Blythe fluttered her eyelashes. "The pleasure was mine."

He gave Amy a nod which indicated she could carry on, and handed over the medical record. The entire episode surprised her so much she couldn't tear her attention away from him. Only after the door closed with a quiet snick was she able to focus once again on her patient.

"Isn't he wonderful?" Blythe gushed. "So nice. So polite."

"Yes, isn't he?"

If Blythe had heard her sarcasm, she didn't show it. "I feel so much better now that I've had a second opinion. Will you make the appointment with the specialist, or shall I?"

"Tess will arrange it and call you with the date and time," Amy said. "And I'll write out your prescription."

"Would you call it in for me, dearie? I have a tendency to lose little pieces of paper." She pointed to her voluminous bag that sat in the corner.

"Sure. What pharmacy?"

"Taylor's," Blythe said, referring to the drugstore owned by a local man with the same name.

Amy scribbled the diagnosis on the billing form along with a request for a urology consult. She also circled the tests she'd performed so Tess could send the necessary charges to the insurance company for reimbursement. "Here you go. Be sure you drink plenty of water."

"I will."

After sending Blythe on her way, she stopped by the receptionist's desk. "Any idea on where my normal saline ended up?"

"Check in Dr Gregory's office. He told Harry to wait to move the second cabinet until you had time to find it a home."

Strange how she hadn't noticed it when she'd barged in earlier. Then again, she'd found his presence so disconcerting that she wouldn't have noticed a grizzly bear if one had been standing in the corner.

This time she approached the doorway more cautiously.

To her relief, he was gone, although his scent hung in the air as a reminder that possession of this particular space had changed hands.

Somewhat resentful over her loss and eager to leave before Ryan returned, she retrieved a bottle of normal saline from the cabinet. As she did so, she was struck by a sudden urge to see what mark he'd made in her former territory.

His desk already showed signs of clutter, but the only personal item was a coffee-cup emblazoned with a picture of the nation's Capitol building. On the far wall, framed five-by-seven photos of various historic Washington, DC sites were grouped around a prominent one of Arlington National Cemetery.

Knowing her patient was waiting, she didn't take time to consider the significance or to search for more clues into his character.

"I'm back," she told Dean a minute later, her supplies in hand. Seeing Dr Gregory in the room chatting away with the real-estate agent, she stopped short.

Afraid he would comment about the delay, she immediately apologized. "Sorry it took me so long," she told Dean, handing him the kidney basin so she could irrigate his affected eye.

He shrugged. "Dr Gregory and I were just passing the time."

She forced her attention on her patient when she would much rather have glared at the doctor in question. "How nice."

Ryan interrupted. "Were you planning to check his cornea?"

"If I can find a slit lamp," she replied.

"We don't have one?"

"I don't think so, but I haven't needed to use that particular piece of equipment before now. I'm hoping Dr Jackson's office can help."

"I'll ask." With that, Ryan left.

She was almost surprised that he hadn't sent her to look and taken care of the patient himself. Mulling over his actions, she began to flush Dean's eye with the saline.

"I had no idea that our new MD is a soccer whiz," Dean mentioned.

"He is?"

That explained his obvious lack of body fat. He probably ran a gazillion miles a day to stay in shape. It was all she could do to take Mindy on a leisurely two-mile stroll each evening. She enjoyed walking, but her cocker spaniel wasn't much of a conversationalist. Other than a few woofs, the effort was a rather lonely pursuit. On the other hand, her aerobics class was filled with chattering women, peppy music and much laughter to make the time zoom by.

"You didn't know?"

"I just met him for the first time yesterday," she admitted. "He'd interviewed for this position before I started working here a month ago, so we never crossed paths until now. Needless to say, we haven't had time to discuss anything personal."

"I'm on the Recreation Commission board and we're always looking for coaches for our youth leagues. Do you suppose he'd be interested in taking on a team?"

"I couldn't begin to guess." Somehow, Dr Gregory didn't seem the type who'd enjoy being around children, but if he'd taken the time to learn how to pull quarters out of thin air, he might.

"How's the family?" she asked, remembering them from her days in Dr Garrett's practice.

"Tony's getting his learner's permit so I can teach him how to drive. I'm not sure I'm ready to hand over the car keys, though. It seems like I bought his tricycle only yesterday."

"They grow up fast," she commented.

"I'll say. Gertie says Tony and his friends are eating us out of house and home."

Amy laughed. "The lament of every parent with a teen-age boy."

The door opened and in walked Dr Gregory, carrying a loupe and several small vials. "We're in luck," he said, sounding satisfied with himself.

"I'm almost finished." Amy handed Dean a towel to blot his face dry.

Ryan held out two vials. "Do you want to do the honors, or shall I?"

His eagerness was palpable and she wondered if he thought she was out of her depth. At least he'd asked her permission. He could have easily pushed her aside and taken charge. Feeling slightly charitable because of his courtesy, she acquiesced. "Be my guest."

After placing two drops of an anesthetic in Dean's eye, he opened the package containing a fluorescein strip and moistened the end with a drop of sterile saline. After touching the strip to the inner edge of Dean's lower eyelid, he said, "Blink your eyes a few times."

Amy knew that blinking would distribute the dye which would stain any foreign bodies and make abrasions more apparent. A few minutes later, Dr Gregory put his borrowed equipment to use.

Meanwhile, Amy busied herself with the cleanup and tried not to dwell on how his presence had caused the room to shrink.

Before long, he flipped off his penlight and straightened. "Everything looks fine. Amy will write a prescription for antibiotic drops. Use them for ten days."

"I will," Dean said.

Dr Gregory crossed the small room to the sink where he washed his hands.

"Any chance you'd be interested in coaching youth soccer?" Dean asked.

He dried his hands on a paper towel while he apologized in what sounded like a sincere tone. "I'm not sure I'll have time this fall. Check with me next season."

"Will do," Dean said cheerfully.

While he and Dr Gregory went in opposite directions, Amy stopped at her desk to call in Blythe's prescription. A handful of messages were already stuck to her blotter, waiting for her attention. She left all of them, except for the one from Dora Wells.

"Dora," she exclaimed once her call went through. "I have a proposition for you."

Dora, a nurse in her late forties, laughed aloud. "What worthy cause are you promoting this time?"

"My own. I'm working with Dr Gregory now—"

"Isn't he the new guy I read about and saw a photo of in the paper? The one who's good-looking in a serious sort of way?"

"Yes. Anyway, we need a nurse in the office and I thought I'd give you first dibs on it, if you're interested."

"Am I," Dora said fervently. "I've been wondering how we'll afford to send Dallas to college. The hospital offered to upgrade me from part-time to full-time hours but the position is on the three-to-eleven shift. I'll hardly ever get the chance to be a sports mom for my other two kids."

"You shouldn't have that problem here," Amy said. "I'm sure we can manage to cover for you if you have to leave early."

"Sold!" Dora said happily. "Where do I sign?"

Amy grinned. "Come in and talk to Dr Gregory. Mind you, he's the one with the final say, but I've already put in a good word for you."

"Geez. I'm impressed."

"What do you mean?"

"Sounds like you've already wrapped him around your little finger."

"Hardly," she answered dryly. If Dora only knew... "He's not the type."

After arranging for Dora to stop by the next day, Amy sat back in her chair and mentally patted herself on the back. Not only was Dora an excellent nurse, but she got along with some of the more high-strung physicians in town. She could easily deal with Dr Gregory.

Now, if she could only say the same for herself.

By the end of the day, Amy felt as worn out as the shoe Mindy liked to chew. Tess didn't look much better.

"Funny how I never felt this frazzled when it was just the two of us," Tess confided.

"You're entitled to," Amy told her as she sat on the corner of Tess's desk and leaned her head against the wall. "We've seen nearly twice as many patients."

Tess groaned. "Don't I know it. I haven't had a chance to file a thing and I can't stay late to catch up."

"Maybe we should hire a filing clerk."

"Pat won't approve a full-time person," Tess warned. "Not after one day."

Amy thought a moment. "Probably not, but she might OK a high-school student who can work a few hours every afternoon. Isn't your daughter old enough to work?"

Tess beamed. "Absolutely. She turned sixteen last month and is going through a stage that's about to drive me to drink. She's constantly in a snit about something. A job is just what she needs."

"Do you think so?"

"If she worked here, she'd see people who are worse off than she thinks she is."

"Then talk to Pat."

"I will." Tess straightened her desk and shut off the computer. "What are you doing this evening?"

Amy slid off the desk. "I thought I'd stick around and figure out where to move the cabinet that's still in Dr Gregory's office."

"It was nice of him to let it stay where it was for now."

"It would have been even nicer if he'd taken the office at the end of the hallway," Amy corrected. To his credit, he hadn't complained on those occasions when she'd walked in to help herself to the supplies.

"I'd offer to lend you a hand, but Carrie has an R2D2 ball game this evening."

Dr Gregory walked by the open doorway and stopped. "Did I hear you say R2D2 baseball?"

Tess nodded. "They set a machine to pitch, which is where they got the name."

"Sounds interesting. Have a good time."

Tess laughed. "I can sure tell *you* don't have any kids. Other than labor and delivery, watching your children compete in sports is the most stressful thing a parent can go through."

A grin slowly spread across his face. It seemed trite to say that it completely transformed him, but to Amy it was nothing short of a miracle. He suddenly seemed like a real person and not a man who was constantly immersed in his work.

"I'll keep that in mind," he said dryly. "For when the day comes."

Tess grabbed her purse. "I'm off. See you two tomorrow."

As soon as she'd left, he glanced at Amy. "Aren't you going home?"

"Not yet. I have a few things to do. Like find a place for the cabinet."

He leaned against the doorjamb as if he wasn't in any big hurry to leave either. "Any ideas?"

"Not really," she said honestly. "I've been too busy to give it much thought."

"Why not use the baby room?" he asked. "They won't care if someone comes in unannounced."

She smiled. "No, I don't imagine they will."

"It's also next door to your nurse's room, so it won't be that much out of your way."

"Sounds like you've given this a lot of thought."

"Not really. I just notice things."

The man should have been an efficiency expert. Still, she couldn't complain. At least he'd had an idea which, on the surface, sounded workable.

Amy started to move past him. "I'll get right on it, then."

"You're not going to move the thing by yourself, are you?"

Surprised and touched by his concern, she shook her head. "I could, but I won't. Eldon and Harry would feel slighted. I'm just going to box up the supplies so the cabinet will be empty for the guys in the morning."

"All right. See you then."

"Good night," she echoed.

As his footsteps faded away, she collapsed into her chair. She'd survived the first day. The rest would surely be easier.

Ryan idly stared at the crates of books stacked against the wall in his living room. Instead of seeing the volumes of obscure subjects he'd collected to fill his quiet hours, he saw Amy Wyman in his mind's eye.

Beautiful, blonde Amy Wyman. His preference tended toward brunettes, but Amy's mane of reddish-blonde hair had made him rethink his tastes. From the moment he'd seen her trim form in the hallway, all thoughts of tending to business had flown out of his head.

After overhearing her comment about jumping all over him, work-related issues had definitely taken a back seat in his thoughts. The mental picture it had evoked had been wickedly appealing and had popped into his head every time he'd seen her throughout the day. Yet he didn't feel remorse for the direction his imagination had traveled. He wasn't made of stone.

He smiled, recalling how reluctant she'd been to face him. Her reaction hadn't been unusual since she'd known that he'd overheard her unflattering remarks. But even as he stared at her from behind and appreciated the view that he hadn't expected, he'd been impatient to see her face to face.

It had been worth the wait.

The description recorded in her personnel folder revealed only the basics. In real life, however, those basics were clearly understated.

She wasn't a classic beauty, but his male instinct whispered that this was a woman who attracted second—and third—glances. Her full lower lip was far too enticing and her corn silk-fine hair begged to be loosed from the tight confines at the back of her head. However, the bounce in her step and the life shining out of her blue-green eyes probably drew men's attention the most. It certainly drew his.

Pacific Ocean blue, he'd decided as he'd stared into those stormy depths. He'd expected her to apologize for her remarks or at least turn pink with chagrin. Instead, she'd raised her chin slightly in a defiant gesture and hadn't flinched under his gaze.

No shrinking violet here, he thought. Then again, from yesterday's conversation, he didn't expect her to be. Yet he was the one who was ultimately responsible for everything in his practice and he refused to ignore that obligation. An adage from one of his instructors came to mind. *Start as you mean to go on.*

He had. He'd outlined his expectations and had begun to implement the changes he thought necessary to promote efficiency. Granted, some were major, if Amy's tight jaw and clenched fists were any indication, but he hadn't expected her to object so strenuously to moving her nurse's room. Yes, she'd arranged it nicely, but with two of them sharing this suite they couldn't afford to waste any space.

Perhaps he should have waited a few days before he reorganized, but he didn't see any sense in postponing the inevitable. It seemed ridiculous to move twice—once into the office down the hall, then again to the room he preferred—just so he could break the news to her gently.

To her credit, she hadn't used any feminine wiles to persuade him to change his mind. If she had, she would have soon learned that he wasn't a pushover for a pretty face or a pouty mouth, no matter how badly he wanted to taste those lips. Fluttering those baby blues wouldn't do much good either, except to get a prescription for eye drops or a referral to a neurologist.

Immediately, he pushed aside the thought. Amy Wyman didn't seem the type to resort to such obvious tactics. From their brief and slightly heated encounters, he'd guessed her to have come by the reddish highlights in her hair naturally. Although he normally avoided interpersonal conflicts, he almost looked forward to the stimulating conversation that was sure to result from their confrontations.

Something told him there would be many.

# CHAPTER FOUR

AMY kicked off her tennis shoes, sank into the overstuffed burgundy chair in her living room and finger-combed her hair out of its tight mooring. It had been a long week and now that Friday had finally arrived she felt as if she'd been pulled through a knothole backward.

At the moment, she couldn't decide if her exhaustion was more physical or mental. Trying to act as Dr Gregory's nurse to his patients while dealing with her own had certainly kept her hopping. She could have put a pair of roller blades to good use. Thank goodness Dora would start in another week. Five more days of doing the job of two people was about all she could stand.

Actually, she wasn't being totally honest. Having to be in two places at once happened more often than not in her practice. One simply had to be capable of being quick, recalling details at a split second's notice and making instant and accurate decisions. It was all part and parcel of this profession.

What *really* bothered her, and what *really* had caused her mind-numbing exhaustion had been having to contend with Dr Gregory.

He had seemed to be everywhere at once. She didn't know how many times she'd been speaking to someone and had turned around to find him at her elbow. He'd dropped in on her patients to introduce himself and she'd never known if he'd leave as quietly as he'd appeared, or if he'd stay and oversee her diagnosis.

Fortunately, he'd always seemed satisfied with her treatment plans but in the meantime her emotions had seesawed between anxiety and relief. As she sprawled bonelessly in the chair, it was obvious how the resultant stress had taken its toll.

Pam's advice, although well meant, had contributed to her strain. Considering how she was a forthright person, biting back her objections and holding her comments had created a granddaddy of a tension headache. She didn't like to mince words or prevaricate, and her utter weariness was clearly the price her body exacted for going against her nature.

Truthfully speaking, she couldn't tell if she had made headway in her cause to prove herself capable. Dr Gregory hadn't seemed to be underfoot quite as often by the end of the week—an encouraging thought—but she sensed that his sharp eye hadn't dimmed at all.

She simply had to be patient. For her, however, that particular trait came in short supply.

A loud woof and scratching on the patio door reminded her of one creature who trusted her implicitly. She padded into the kitchen and saw Mindy sitting on the concrete step with her nose pressed against the glass. After skirting the dining table to reach the door, she slid it open and crouched to hug the wiggling mass of fur.

"How were you today, Mindy?" she crooned.

Mindy answered with a series of licks to Amy's face and a bark for good measure.

"Shall we skip our walk tonight? It's still ninety degrees outside."

With her tail wagging, Mindy ran to the living room doorway and peered back at Amy with a question in her doggy eyes.

"There's an extra biscuit in it for you if we stay at home and relax," Amy coaxed, but her pet was oblivious to her bribe.

Amy rose. "All right, you silly girl. Let me change clothes first."

Mindy barked again, apparently agreeable to her mistress's plan.

Amy exchanged her uniform for a pair of dark green athletic shorts and a sleeveless green and white top. She gathered her hair at her nape with a rubber band and slipped on her walking shoes. After grabbing last night's newspaper and hooking Mindy's leash to her collar, she let the cocker spaniel lead her out of the house.

While Mindy's toenails clicked against the concrete at a sedate pace, Amy marveled at how she'd found the place of her dreams in the town's newest housing development. Considering her love of water, the Great Lakes had seemed a fitting place for her. Each street was appropriately named after one of the lakes, although the closest thing to a body of water—other than a backyard swimming pool—was a duck pond in a nearby park. In any event, the two-bedroom house on Ontario had met her needs and, better yet, her price range.

Because the area was filled with starter homes, her neighbors were mostly single with a few newlyweds thrown in for good measure. Sometimes the party-hearty crowd grew tiresome, but all in all she was surrounded by enough people who kept her life from being dull.

And speaking of dull, she wanted nothing more than to go home and soak her troubles away in a tub full of hot water and scented bubbles. If she was able to summon the energy later, she might drop in on Jodie Mitchell's barbecue.

Amy followed the course Mindy had set for the park. A few minutes later, she unhooked the leash before sending the rolled newspaper into the air for Mindy to fetch.

About a hundred yards away in a grassy area a group of

men were playing soccer. Instantly, she thought of Dr Gregory, but she didn't recognize him in the crowd.

Don't be ridiculous, she told herself firmly, throwing the newspaper farther. It was Friday night and she didn't want to think of the doctor until Monday morning.

As soon as Mindy appeared to tire of their game, Amy attached the leash and they headed for home. After she'd settled Mindy in the kitchen with her bowl of dog food and had poured herself a tall glass of lemonade, Amy stared across her yard to the house directly behind hers.

Most homes in this development were built to similar specifications although the exterior paint varied. While hers was light blue with dark blue shutters, the one across the way was cream-colored with dark brown trim. It had been vacant for the past two weeks after the previous owners had moved to Iowa, but now she could see lights inside. The Claytons had spoiled Mindy terribly and she hoped her newest backyard neighbor would be as friendly as they had been.

Her doorbell rang and she ruffled Mindy's ears before she went to answer.

Jodie, a gorgeous redhead who worked at the local television station, stood on the porch. She wore tight black capri pants and a skimpy green knit shirt that bared her flat stomach. A chunky gold necklace, long hoop earrings and strappy gold high-heeled sandals accessorized her ensemble.

"You're coming to my party, aren't you?" she asked as she crossed the threshold.

"Later," Amy prevaricated. "After I soak in the tub for a few hours."

"Can you cut it back to about fifteen minutes? I need a favor."

Inwardly Amy groaned. Jodie was as sweet as punch, but Amy swore that "favor" was her middle name. "I know. You forgot to buy ice and need me to bring a few bags.''

The redhead smiled a feline sort of grin. ''I had something much hotter in mind.''

''Don't you think it's a little warm for coffee?''

''No, no, no,'' Jodie said, waving her hands and shaking her head for emphasis. ''I meant hot in another sense.'' She wiggled her eyebrows.

''Hot'' in Jodie's terminology usually referred to the male half of the species. Amy couldn't possibly imagine what sort of favor she'd be called upon to deliver. ''It's been a long week. You'd better spell it out for me.''

Jodie tapped her sandal-clad foot and threw up her hands impatiently. ''I met your new neighbor a little while ago and invited him to my party. I want you to bring him with you.''

''Surely he can find his own way,'' Amy said wryly. ''All he has to do is step into his backyard and he'll see everyone two doors down.''

''Yes, but I have a feeling he won't come by himself. He doesn't seem like a socializer, if you know what I mean.''

''If he doesn't want to come—'' Amy began.

''What better way for him to meet his neighbors?'' Jodie asked stubbornly. ''This is for his own good. Everyone needs to know who lives nearby. He might need to borrow a cup of sugar some time.''

Amy rolled her eyes. ''Then *you* can escort him over.''

Jodie was aghast. ''And risk making Wayne jealous? Not a chance. He's been moody enough lately.''

The bubbles in Amy's mental bath were starting to disappear. ''Surely you could ask someone else…''

Jodie's gold hoops swung like pendulums as she shook her head. ''It has to be you. You have a real gift for drawing people out of their shells so they can relax and enjoy themselves. Besides, what man would turn down a chance to have a beautiful, vivacious blonde on his arm?''

Amy sniggered at the ''beautiful'' comment. She considered herself attractive, but beautiful? Hardly.

Jodie hesitated for only a fraction of a second. ''Puleeze,'' she wheedled.

Amy's resolve wavered. Her bubble bath was slowly turning into a shower before her very eyes. A very *short* shower, if she fell in line with Jodie's plans.

''And all I have to do is walk him over to the party.'' Amy didn't want any last-minute surprises, like the time she'd been roped into coming over for dinner and had ended up rounding out a foursome at bridge. It wouldn't have been so bad, but she hadn't known the first thing about the game. After more hands than she cared to remember, she still struggled with the basics.

''Well…'' Jodie had the grace to avoid Amy's direct gaze. ''I'm hoping you'll introduce him to everyone—steer him toward someone he can talk to. I don't want him feeling like the odd man out. He comes across as rather quiet. A real man of few words.''

''How can I do that if I don't know him either?'' Amy pointed out. ''He may live behind me, but I've never met him. At least you have.''

''You're so good at things like this,'' Jodie insisted. ''With you both being in the medical profession, I figure, if nothing else, you can talk shop.''

After the week she'd had, talking shop was the last way Amy had envisioned spending her evening.

''So what does he do?'' Amy asked, recalling mention of a physical therapist moving to town.

''He's a doctor.''

''A doctor?'' A feeling of impending doom began to flow down to her toes as Jodie's description began to apply to someone else she knew. ''What's his name?''

Jodie screwed her face into a squint. "Greg something or other."

Amy's stomach completely flipped over. "Ryan Gregory?"

Jodie snapped her fingers. "That's it. How did you know?"

"I work with him," she said slowly.

"What a coincidence. You'll have so much in common. Isn't that wonderful?" Jodie beamed with delight.

"Yeah, isn't it?" Clearly Jodie didn't notice how Amy's enthusiasm fell short of her own. At the same time, it seemed petty to ignore him when he lived so close. And if she thought her actions childish, what would *he* think once he arrived and saw her?

She had no choice. She'd help out a friend, but that didn't mean she had to like it. "OK," she said, her tone resigned.

Her mission accomplished, Jodie stepped outside. "Anyway, bring him over as soon as you're ready. We're firing up the grill at seven-thirty, so don't be late."

"Seven-thirty," Amy dutifully replied.

Determined to postpone the inevitable, she took a long, leisurely shower, contemplating the evening ahead. She could easily imagine Dr Gregory staying at home in spite of a personal invitation to the festivities occurring only a few houses away. With her as his escort, she especially had a hard time seeing him unbend enough to enjoy himself. After working together this past week, she'd have described him as a poster child for the adage, "All work and no play makes Jack a dull boy."

But even as the thought crossed her mind, she chided herself for being unfair. It was true; he was serious and not prone to joking around the office. That, however, didn't make him dull in the literal sense of the word. He'd conversed with his patients on a surprisingly diverse array of subjects. With Mrs Pendleton, he'd discussed classical composers; with Blake Landon, he'd talked about stock portfolios, and with the fellow from the local grain co-op, he'd sympathized over the low price of wheat.

No, Ryan Gregory wasn't dull or a social misfit. He obviously had depths to his character that only a few people took time to explore. Although curiosity taunted her to dig beneath his controlled surface and discover what made him tick, she tamped down the feeling. All she wanted was to do her job without hassles. She didn't need to delve into his personal life for that to happen.

Her time of procrastination drew to a close as the water slowly changed from hot to lukewarm. Turning off the taps, she toweled herself dry and slipped into a dressy pair of khaki shorts and a sleeveless moss-green cotton shirt. She blow-dried her hair, swiped blush across her cheeks, inserted a pair of tiny silver hoops in her earlobes and splashed on her favorite cologne before she declared herself ready.

Mentally, however, she was far from it.

All you have to do is introduce him to the neighbors, she told her reflection in the full-length hall mirror. Then he was on his own.

"Wish me luck," she told Mindy as she scratched behind the spaniel's ears. "Do you want in or out?"

Mindy stayed on her rug and thumped her tail on the floor.

"In it is. Don't wait up."

Mindy replied by laying her head on her two front paws and yawning.

"Lucky dog," she said affectionately before she stepped onto her patio. Already she could hear music in the distance with an occasional burst of laughter and a splash of water as someone dived into the pool. Jodie's guests had arrived.

If this had been a more formal occasion than a backyard

barbecue and pool party, she might have considered walking the extra steps to Dr Gregory's front entrance, but it wasn't and so she didn't. Instead, she slipped through the gate in the chain-link fence separating their properties, hurried across the recently mowed grass, climbed the four steps of his wooden deck and strode with determination toward the sliding glass patio door.

Taking a deep breath for courage, she raised her hand to rap sharply on the metal frame. Before she could do so, she saw him standing on the other side, wearing dark brown dress shorts and a cream-colored polo shirt.

She forced a smile, hoping it was bright enough to hide her dread. She wanted so badly to turn tail and run for home, but the die had been cast. She had to grit her teeth and see her part in Jodie's unholy plan to completion.

Ryan could hardly believe his eyes as his nurse-practitioner marched from the opposite yard into his. He'd had no idea that Amy lived in the neighborhood, much less that she'd lived within a stone's throw.

He'd talked himself out of going to the barbecue, then had changed his mind in the interests of good public relations. These people were neighbors after all. However, that didn't mean he wanted to spend his entire evening drinking beer and listening to loud music. His plan had been to ask his answering service to page him at eight-thirty, giving him a valid excuse to leave.

Seeing Amy, however, he was glad he hadn't made the call yet. Obviously, she would be at this little bash and he could try to make amends for how hard he'd pushed her this past week. To be honest, though, if coming across as the bad guy kept her on her toes, then feeling guilty for doing so was a small price to pay.

The woman who worked in his office bore little resemblance to the one who'd just ascended the stairs of his deck. After seeing her as a mischievous clown, a prim NP with a pen stuck in her tight bun and now a sexy young woman with hair floating around her shoulders like a cloud of cotton candy, he was totally intrigued.

Amy Wyman was plainly as changeable as the seasons.

He slid open the door. "This is a surprise," he welcomed her with a smile. "I had no idea you lived around here."

"For about six months," she said.

"Then the tan cocker spaniel is yours?"

"Her name is Mindy. She's not keeping you awake at night, is she?"

She sounded almost worried, as if she was afraid he'd complain to the police or the humane society. "No, but she's a friendly pup. Every time I walk outside, she rushes to the fence and begs for a scratch."

Her laughter reminded him of music. "That's Mindy all right. She's always on the lookout for a new pal or a dog biscuit."

In her next breath the conversation changed. "Jodie asked me to make sure you found your way to her party."

He took a pointed glance in the direction of their destination. "Doesn't say much for my navigating skills."

Amy's face took on a pinkish tinge. "It wasn't a question of you getting lost."

"She was afraid I wouldn't come if left to my own devices," he guessed.

A distinct sparkle made Amy's blue eyes shimmer like sunlight off water. "Was she right?"

A full smile tugged on his mouth. "Yes and no." He didn't elaborate and she didn't press for details.

"Everyone wants to meet you."

"Really?" This was what he hated about starting over—this feeling of being on display like a storefront mannequin.

She nodded. "We're a close-knit group."

He motioned her inside and closed the door behind her. "So I can expect people to be dropping by all the time."

"Not *all* the time," she corrected. "It's more a case of people stopping to chat if you're outside, mowing your grass or washing your car."

Her explanation didn't make it sound as awful as he'd anticipated.

"So," she continued, "did you want to go to Jodie's party? If not, I'll make your excuses."

She plainly wasn't going to beg him to attend. If he were in her shoes, he probably wouldn't want to spend a free evening with him either. "What would you tell them?" he asked, curious.

"You're a doctor. No one will question if you're called for an emergency."

"Except if it was obvious that I hadn't left my house," he pointed out.

"True." She grinned. "You could sit in the dark."

"No fun if you're alone." It would be another story if *she* were with him, but he wouldn't admit to such a thought.

"Then what's your decision?"

"In the interests of neighborhood peace, I'll go. At least for a little while," he qualified. "Do I need to bring something?"

"Only yourself."

"I have an unopened bottle of wine in the fridge," he said, thinking aloud.

She cocked her head as if to study him. "You drink wine? You don't seem the type."

He was amused by her reaction. "I don't?"

"No. Scotch and soda. Martinis. Hard stuff."

He must have outdone himself in the harsh department this week. "Actually, I rarely drink liquor. The wine is strictly for special occasions and medicinal purposes. Red wine promotes a healthy heart, you know."

"Tonight you can take off your doctor coat," she informed him. "Jodie's notorious for her food. Every bite is guaranteed to clog a few arteries, but your taste buds won't let you care."

Thinking of the frozen dinner awaiting him, Ryan was more than ready to raise his cholesterol level. "If I leave my so-called doctor coat at home, will you call me Ryan?"

"Deal."

He smiled and gestured for her to precede him. "Then what are we waiting for?"

With the bottle of wine in hand, he escorted Amy outside. The music filling the evening air was vintage rock and roll and it grew louder as he followed Amy through the maze of gates which allowed them access from one yard to another. A distinct aroma of meat sizzling on a grill suddenly made him realize how long ago lunch had been.

As she pushed open the final gate, he instinctively braced himself to endure one of the big parties that he thoroughly disliked. If the look of delight on Amy's face at the sight of the crowd was any indication, she thrived on these events. From the way people responded with cheery hellos and broad smiles as soon as she appeared, they were equally pleased to see her.

As she grabbed his hand and led him forward to the first group of people, he forced himself to act calmly. Rather than think about remembering names and faces, he concentrated on the feel of her small hand fitting perfectly in his.

For an odd moment he wanted to backtrack and enjoy a quiet evening getting to know Amy rather than the neighbors.

The only other person he recognized was Jodie, and she descended upon them immediately. "You came!"

He smiled. "You sent the cavalry. I couldn't refuse." He held out the bottle. "This is for you."

"You shouldn't have," she exclaimed as she accepted his gift. "But thanks. Help yourself to whatever you want. Wayne is manning the keg of beer and there's soft drinks in the ice chest.'' With a wiggle of her fingers, she disappeared.

Ryan turned to Amy. ''Is she always like this?''

She smiled. ''Pretty much. She can't seem to sit still. Come on. I'll introduce you.''

For the next hour, Amy steered Dr Gregory—no, *Ryan*, she corrected herself—to everyone in attendance. Although he politely conversed with each one, answering their questions calmly, by the time they'd made the rounds his face appeared somewhat strained.

She didn't blame him. The questions had ranged from everything concerning his origins to his current love life. She was worn out by the inquisition, so she could imagine how trying he'd found the situation.

It was time for the comfort of food. ''Now you can relax,'' she said as she handed him a paper plate. Her agreed-upon job was technically over, but she felt strangely unwilling to leave him on his own as she'd originally planned. Somewhere in the middle of her Jodie-appointed task, she'd started seeing him not as her taciturn boss but as an interesting individual. She didn't know how her new perspective would affect her life come Monday, but she'd worry about it then. For now, she'd enjoy herself and see that he did, too.

''Do you think so?'' he asked. ''I was almost afraid the last lady was going to ask to see my teeth.''

Amy laughed. ''Eve is always on the lookout for a prospective son-in-law. Once you admitted that you were single, I saw the glint in her eye.''

''Yeah, I did, too. I was praying my beeper would go off. Where's an emergency when you need one?'' he mourned.

''Then that *was* a look of relief I saw on your face when I suggested we move on?'' she teased.

''Absolutely. I'm forever grateful.''

"I aim to please," she replied.

"We have quite an interesting bunch of neighbors," he commented as he scanned the crowd scattered around the pool.

"You think so?"

He nodded. "If I accepted everybody's offers for fishing, going to the lake, bowling, ball games and so on, I wouldn't work until some time in October."

"They're just trying to include you," she said lightly. "Make you feel welcome."

"I appreciate the gesture." He motioned across the yard. "Speaking of interesting, I'd say Wayne has tended the keg a little too closely this evening."

Amy glanced in the direction he'd indicated. Wayne, a divorced fellow in his early forties who was currently keeping company with Jodie, was weaving drunkenly along the far edge of the rectangular pool, flailing his arms.

"How odd," Amy said aloud. "He normally doesn't drink to excess—" Before she could finish her thought, Wayne clutched his throat, slipped on the wet edge and fell into the water.

Those nearby laughed, but Amy didn't. Something was wrong. Wayne wasn't trying to save himself.

Hearing Ryan mutter a curse under his breath, she started forward only to hear a splash and find that Ryan had dived in. While Amy rushed along the edge, he executed a perfect breaststroke to reach the victim in less time than it took her to force her way through the crowd.

She knelt on the side where Ryan was towing Wayne in the classic rescue hold. The laughter stopped as if someone had pulled a plug. A hush spread through the group while the disembodied voice from the CD continued to sing of lost love.

"Shut that off," Amy commanded as she grabbed the

collar of Wayne's shirt and pulled while Ryan guided him through the water.

Suddenly a multitude of hands was there to help and soon Wayne was lying on the concrete. His lips were blue and his face pale. She pressed her fingers against his carotid artery and watched for respirations. A second later, Ryan was dripping beside her.

"There's a faint pulse. No respirations," she reported, checking Wayne's airway.

"Did anyone see what happened?" Ryan asked.

"He was eating," one of the men reported. "He was telling a joke about two chickens, so when he got up and started acting funny…we thought it was part of his act."

Jodie pushed her way into their inner circle. "What's wrong with him?"

"He may have choked on something." Ryan barked another order. "Move back."

Amy and the rest of the crowd obeyed as he began abdominal thrusts. If Wayne had indeed choked on his food, which had started the series of events leading to him falling in the pool, Ryan would have to remove the object before their resuscitation efforts would be successful.

Nothing happened.

"Get him up," Ryan ordered. The men around them lifted Wayne like a rag doll so Ryan could stand behind him and perform the Heimlich maneuver.

Several thrusts later, a piece of meat flew out of Wayne's mouth like a projectile. A little water followed. In the next instant, air rushed into Wayne's lungs and he started to cough.

"Lay him down," Ryan commanded.

Again, an array of helping hands lowered Wayne to the cement, placing him on his side on Ryan's instructions. "Can you hear me, Wayne?"

Wayne nodded once.

"Does your chest hurt?" Ryan asked.

"Some."

"Can you talk?"

"Yeah." Wayne sounded hoarse. "Throat's sore."

"I'll bet it is. Just relax, buddy," Ryan told him. "You'll be OK."

"Feel stupid," he muttered.

"You should," Jodie scolded, her voice tearful as she rubbed his shoulder. "Choking on a piece of hamburger and nearly drowning to boot. Just see if I don't purée everything you eat from now on."

"Holy moly, woman!" Wayne replied weakly. "It could have happened to anyone."

Jodie grabbed his hand. "But it didn't."

"Hey, Doc?" Wayne asked. "Can I sit up now?"

"Sure." Ryan helped him to a sitting position. "How are you feeling?"

"Fine. Can't we just get back to the party?"

With the drama over, the hush disappeared as everyone discussed amongst themselves what had happened.

"Sure, but just sit here until you're strong enough to walk," Ryan told him. "You've had quite a shock and your body hasn't adjusted yet."

Wayne nodded. "No kidding. My legs are weak."

"We wouldn't want you falling into the pool again," Amy teased.

Jodie's face still showed her concern. "Are you sure he's all right? He still looks pale."

"It might be a good idea to go to the emergency room," Ryan suggested. "I doubt if you aspirated any fluid into your lungs as the meat blocked your airway, but I'd advise you to make the trip. After you change clothes."

"I'm OK," Wayne insisted, his voice stronger, although he wiped his forehead with a shaky hand. His brown hair lay plastered against his head.

Amy grabbed a few of the towels lying nearby and handed one to each man. "You'll feel better after you've dried off a little."

"Thanks," Ryan said, draping his over his head.

"Say, guys," someone called out, "don't you know you're supposed to wear swimming trunks in the pool?"

"We're setting a new trend," Ryan countered dryly. As their laughter broke the tension, he addressed Wayne again. "If you start to have chest pain or trouble breathing, say something. We'll be here if you need us."

As he left Wayne's side, most followed his example. Before long, the sound of laughter mingled with the music as the former light-hearted atmosphere returned.

"Why don't you run home and change?" Amy suggested.

Ryan slung the towel around his neck. "It's warm outside. I'll dry fast. Wayne and Jodie would probably feel better if we didn't leave yet."

His consideration for their feelings at the expense of his own comfort touched her. He didn't seem like the same man who'd warned her to watch her step.

Ryan refilled his plate of goodies. "I must admit, this has been quite a party."

Amy laughed. "It's certainly been most memorable."

An hour later, Amy's adrenaline rush had faded and her exhaustion once again tugged at her. "It looks as if everyone is staying," she told Ryan, "but I'm going to slip away. It's been a long day."

"I'll walk you home," he said.

"Now who can't find their way?" she teased.

He grinned. "One never knows what dangers lie hidden in the shadows."

"It's barely dusk."

"Yeah, but I'm ready to call it quits, too. My shorts are still on the damp side." He thanked Jodie for the invitation and quietly unlatched the gate before anyone else noticed they were leaving.

"Things turned out rather well, considering," Amy said as they retraced their steps home.

"Thanks for bringing me along."

"Even though you had to slip on your doctor coat?"

He shrugged. "It took long enough to earn. I don't mind wearing it."

"I bet you'll get invited to all the parties now."

He groaned. "I hope not."

"Why? You don't like mingling with people, eating a smorgasbord of good food and hearing great music?"

"I don't *dis*like parties," he said. "There are just other things I'd rather do."

Amy stopped at the border of their yards. "Like what?" she asked, noticing the slight curl in his hair since the breeze had blown it dry.

Ryan hesitated as if unsure of himself. "Like this."

With that, he bent his head and kissed her.

# CHAPTER FIVE

AMY had been kissed a number of times in her life but Ryan's kiss somehow made those occasions seem insignificant. Electricity hummed through her veins until she thought she'd burst into flame. Her brain lost all ability for rational thought as a sea of sensations surrounded her.

She closed her eyes to the blue and pink hues created by the setting sun and concentrated only on the world within arm's reach.

A faint chlorine odor clung to Ryan's clothes but she easily distinguished his natural male scent as she stood within his embrace. His muscles were hard under her hands and his warmth surrounded her like a well-fitting glove. She slid her palms upward, feeling the cords in his neck before she ran her fingers through the soft strands of his hair.

Serenaded by the nighttime sounds of crickets and cicadas, she tasted sugar and spice on his lips. As his hands drew her against his full length, she had a vague realization of how well they fitted together.

Something hot and heavy seemed to surge between them and his gentle embrace took on more passionate overtones. His hands moved restlessly over her body, stroking, caressing, creating a desire in her that begged for completion.

A barking dog brought her out of her haze. The pressure of his mouth slowly eased, although his heat continued to surround her. As she opened her eyes, a star winked into existence above him, making her feel as if she, too, had undergone a subtle awakening.

Her sense of well-being suddenly turned into chagrin. What was she thinking?

As if he sensed her doubts, he loosened his hold. "*That* was what I'd wanted to do."

She managed to swallow. Although she prided herself on her ability to adapt to whatever situation she found herself in, his kiss had totally thrown her off balance. "It was?"

"Yes." He lifted the latch to her gate. "You'd better go inside."

"I should?" Mercy sakes, she still sounded dazed and breathless.

He nudged her gently through the opening. "You should," he affirmed. "Otherwise I'll do something unwise and invite you in for coffee."

"What's wrong with coffee?"

He smiled. "We wouldn't be drinking coffee. We wouldn't be drinking *anything*, unless you're staying for breakfast."

Ryan's implication was obvious. She was grateful that the growing darkness hid the blush now warming her cheeks.

"It would complicate our lives," she admitted. In fact, this one kiss had already done so.

The gate squeaked as he closed and latched it. That simple act served to distance them and she didn't fail to note its significance. A sense of loss crept over her, filling her with deep regret.

"Good night, Amy," he said softly. "Sleep well."

Having tasted heaven but not enjoying all it had to offer, she doubted if she could.


On Saturday, Ryan sat on his deck and read the paper as he drank his usual cup of coffee. Although the day promised to be another warm one, for the moment he didn't want to waste the morning sun's rays by being indoors. More important, he didn't want to miss an opportunity to talk to his neighbor.

A few minutes later, his wait paid off. Amy slid open her glass patio door and Mindy trotted outside for a sniff of the yard and a stop at her favorite corner. Meanwhile, Amy refilled the water dish from the spigot and served Mindy's breakfast out of the bowl she carried, yawning as she did so. Clearly, she'd just crawled out of bed. And if that were the case, then she probably slept in the white boxer shorts and skin-tight top that exposed her waistline.

Talk about a sight for sore eyes.

"Morning!" he called as he folded the daily newspaper.

She turned to face him. The smile on her face came slowly as she ran both hands through her tousled hair. Her shirt slid upward and his mouth went dry at the sight of her luscious curves straining against the fabric.

The telephone company's catchy jingle to advertise their Yellow Pages—"Let your fingers do the walking"—suddenly took on an entirely new meaning. He wished now that he hadn't been so chivalrous in sending her home alone last night. Logically, it had been the right thing to do. His few romantic relationships had been notoriously short-lived and having one with his delectable nurse-practitioner would, as she'd already admitted, be unwise.

Too bad she didn't work with Jackson.

"Hi," she answered.

He strolled down the steps to the gate separating their properties. "Any word from Jodie or Wayne?"

"No. He must have been feeling OK because things didn't wind down until around two a.m."

It had been two-fifteen, but Ryan didn't correct her. Apparently she'd had as much trouble going to sleep as he'd had. His excuse, though, had nothing to do with the noise. Every time he'd closed his eyes, Amy had filled his thoughts. He'd finally resorted to riding his stationary bicycle for hours until he'd been too exhausted to do anything but fall into bed.

Even that, however, hadn't stopped him from dreaming.

Mindy took that moment to bound over to him and stick her nose through the chain links of the fence. Ryan crouched down to pat her head.

"Is she always this friendly?"

"I'm afraid so. The people who lived here before you spoiled her horribly. I'm afraid she thinks you're either going to give her a treat or will open the gate and pet her."

"Sorry, Mindy," he said. "I'm empty-handed. As for petting, I'd be happy to let you visit me." He lifted the latch and Mindy squeaked through the space before he fully opened the gate.

"I can tell that you like dogs. Do you have one?"

Bending over, he scratched Mindy behind the ears before she rolled onto her back to expose her tummy. "I did when I was a kid, but he was a hole-digger. One night, he dug his way out and I never saw him again. So I got a tank full of tropical fish. No chance of them running away." He grinned.

"But they're not as much fun."

He shrugged. "They have their own personalities, too. You just have to be patient and watch."

"Well, Mindy's quite the beggar, so if she bothers you…"

"She won't," he said, already deciding that he liked the spaniel's enthusiasm. "It will be nice to play with her and then send her home to Mama."

Amy giggled. "Just like having grandkids."

"Yeah." Looking at her reminded him of how children had to come first. It also reminded him of how those same children came about. None of these were thoughts he should be dwelling on after a night filled with dreams of Amy.

"Speaking of kids, I have to go," she said, sounding a

trifle reluctant. "I'm baby-sitting Tess's two youngest while she takes her oldest daughter shopping in Topeka."

As energetic as Amy was, the youngsters probably couldn't wait until she arrived. "I won't keep you, then." He called to the spaniel who was checking out the azalea bushes near one fence. "Time to go, Mindy. Come again some time."

The spaniel lifted her head and trotted back into her yard as if she was used to being sent home.

This time, Amy closed the gate. Ryan gripped the top bar, aware of how close she stood. All he had to do was reach out and touch her...

Wishing his athletic shorts had pockets so he could occupy his hands, he stepped backward. "Have a nice weekend."

"Thanks. You, too."

He forced himself to walk away without a backward glance. Yes, she appealed to him on the most elemental level, but he refused to open himself up for more heartbreak. The adage of opposites attracting may have been true, but after his experiences, he didn't trust those relationships to last.

However, on Monday morning, his resolve wavered as Amy walked into the clinic promptly at eight o'clock. "Good morning," she said with a tentative smile.

Her prim uniform was like the outer wrapping of a Christmas package. The shapeless trousers and baggy shirt hid the temptress he'd seen a few days ago. He clutched one end of his stethoscope as if it were a lifeline and forced himself to use his objective doctor voice. "Same to you. How was your weekend?"

"Exhausting. What about you?"

After racking up the miles on his bicycle, he could claim exhaustion, too. "Same here."

Tess poked her head in the hallway. "If you two think

you're going to coast through today, guess again. I've already had three calls for people wanting to be worked in A.S.A.P.''

Amy grinned. "No rest for the wicked. I guess I'd better get things organized.''

Considering how he'd spent a great deal of his weekend thinking wonderfully sinful thoughts, her comment was appropriate. As she disappeared in her nurse's room, one thought flashed through his mind in bright, neon letters.

He was in trouble of the worst kind.

His professional side wanted to monitor her closely, but to do so would wreak havoc with his composure. It was difficult to concentrate on her medical skills when all he wanted was to loosen the knot of hair on her head, unbutton the shapeless puppy-printed uniform top, slip the matching pants down her legs and bury himself in her softness.

His craving was totally out of line. The only way to reel in his thoughts was to limit their physical contact. That, in turn, meant he couldn't keep tabs on her the way he wanted. He might not have found fault with her abilities after scrutinizing nearly everything she'd done this past week, but it didn't signify complete trust in her either.

He simply had to think of a way to resolve his catch-22 situation.

Two weeks later, Amy accepted Pam's invitation to lunch, knowing her friend would press her for the latest update concerning Ryan. As much as she wanted Pam's advice, she wasn't willing to bare her soul. Some details were still too fresh to be shared.

The waitress had just left a bowl of salsa and a basket of tortilla chips before Pam's grilling began.

"How's it going?'' she asked. "Is Dr Gregory still looking over your shoulder?''

"Yes and no,'' Amy replied, swirling a chip in the dip.

"He still drops in on my patients before I can get in the room—don't ask me how he manages to do that when he has his own rooms filled—but now he only does it a couple of times a week."

"How do the patients feel?"

"They're flattered by his attention. I, on the other hand, know what he's doing."

But did she? Ever since that night they'd kissed, she'd expected things to be different. In one respect they were because each time she saw him her mind replayed those few minutes in living color. It was next to impossible to see him in his professional persona when her mental picture portrayed a handsome man with windblown hair against the backdrop of a colorful Kansas sunset.

However, the difference she'd anticipated in their working relationship had never come to fruition. If she hadn't experienced the breathtaking excitement of being in his arms for herself, she would never have known it had happened. He acted just as distant and serious as he had before that night. Her vision of him becoming more relaxed remained just that—a vision. Plainly, he'd compartmentalized his private and his personal life with astonishing success.

If only she could keep the two as separate as he did.

"He's obviously a tougher nut to crack than I'd thought," Pam mused aloud. "Still, it sounds as if he's improving. Just give him time."

"At the rate we're going, he won't fully trust me until I reach retirement age."

Once again, Pam grinned. "You're making progress. Don't be so impatient."

Amy dipped another chip. "Unfortunately, patience is a virtue I don't have."

"Then maybe you should have a heart-to-heart. You've worked together, what? Almost a month now?"

The waitress returned with their taco salads and Amy

waited to answer until she'd left. "Three weeks," she corrected. "I suppose I should discuss this again, but I'm a little nervous."

"You? Nervous about speaking your mind?" Pam shook her head. "What's come over you, girl?"

"Just following your advice," she quipped, keeping the real reason to herself. She'd built a fantasy around Ryan Gregory the man, and she didn't want Ryan Gregory the doctor spoiling it.

"If he doesn't change soon, then it's time to revise the game plan," Pam retorted. "Keep him guessing at all times. Otherwise he'll take you for granted."

"That's just it. I *want* to be taken for granted. I want him to have confidence in me."

"Keep working at it. If water drips long enough, it will wear down a rock."

Unfortunately, she didn't have Mother Nature's patience. After lunch, she returned to the clinic and decided to speak to Ryan as soon as their last patient left. As she passed the receptionist's desk, Tess motioned her forward.

"What's up?" Amy asked.

"You're wanted on line two. Judith Wentworth."

"I'll take it in my office." A minute later, she selected the blinking button. "Hello, Judith. What can I do for you today?"

"Jason's still complaining of a sore throat. I thought I'd ask if you'd had his culture report."

"I haven't seen it, but let me get back to you. Are you at home?"

After promising to call her back shortly, Amy went in search of the lab report. When she couldn't find it, she called the microbiologist and learned the results were positive for strep pneumoniae. According to the drug sensitivity profile, Jason should be responding to her treatment.

Intent on looking for his medical record so she could

document her findings, she was both surprised and puzzled to discover it missing from the stacks.

She fingered the tabbed folders for a third time, hoping—no, *praying*—for the chart to appear. Jason's file was the fourth such incident in the last two weeks and Amy was becoming increasingly frustrated.

Granted, the days had been stressful, but that didn't mean she couldn't do her job or keep her head glued on straight.

There was a logical explanation, she told herself as she continued down the alphabet, still staying with the Ws. The file simply had to be here somewhere.... But by the time she reached ''Wynn'', she had to admit defeat.

''Is there a problem...Amy?'' Ryan's familiar baritone floated over her shoulder.

She swirled to face him. Her concern over the file hadn't impaired her ability to hear the hesitation in his voice before he'd said her name. It was as if he was uncomfortable with such informality, but he didn't seem to have the same difficulty when he addressed anyone else.

Only her.

Pushing that observation to the back of her mind, she wiped the worry off her face. ''A problem? Why would you think that?'' She wasn't about to admit to misplacing a patient record, especially when she *knew* beyond all shadow of a doubt that she'd placed it in the filing bin two nights ago.

Of course, if anyone other than Ryan Gregory had asked her the same question, she would have answered honestly. He'd been waiting for her to make a mistake and if she admitted to misplacing files, she might lose the small amount of progress she'd made.

He stood in the doorway, nonchalantly leaning one hip against the frame. ''You looked a little, shall we say, intense?''

She nearly laughed aloud. Ryan could have given lessons

on the subject. "I was thinking," she said defensively, before she changed the subject. "Did you need something?"

He straightened from his relaxed pose. "Have you seen the results of Rhea Drake's sonogram?"

"Not yet. I'll call if you'd like."

"Ask them to fax the report. Her next prenatal is this afternoon. I'd ask Dora, but she's busy at the moment."

After following through with his request, she phoned Mrs Wentworth. "Jason's throat culture was positive for pneumococcus," Amy told her. "Is he still running a temp?"

"Yes, but the acetominophen is keeping it down fairly well. He's better than what he was, but I was concerned because he normally bounces back once he starts taking medicine."

"He will," Amy reassured her. "Continue with the pain-reliever and make sure he drinks plenty of fluids. You should see noticeable improvement in another twenty-four hours with the antibiotic I've already prescribed."

"I'm glad to hear we're on the right track," Mrs Wentworth said.

Amy documented her phone call on the appropriate form and placed it on her desk. She'd add this note when the missing record appeared, provided the office gremlins had only misplaced it and not made it vanish completely.

Tess stopped at Amy's desk. "Why are you muttering about gremlins?"

"If I didn't know better, I'd think this place was haunted," Amy grumbled, signing her name with a flourish. "I can't find a medical record. Again."

"The Wentworth boy?"

"Yes. I had it a few days ago when I ordered his throat culture. I can't imagine where it might have gone."

"Where did you put the file after his appointment?"

Amy pointed to the table next to the color-coded shelves of records. "Same place they always go. In the bin."

"Then Mollie's already shelved it," Tess decided.

"I've looked. I went through the entire section of Ws in case it was misfiled. No such luck."

"It can't disappear into thin air."

"I agree, but where is it? I've looked every place imaginable."

"As soon as Mollie comes in this afternoon, I'll ask her," Tess said.

"Thanks."

"Don't worry. It'll turn up."

"Not soon enough for me," Amy said, her voice glum. "If this was an isolated incident, I wouldn't be concerned, but it's not."

"I'm sure Mollie will shed some light on this," Tess said. "She has an amazing ability to remember names."

"Let's hope she remembers this one. How's she doing by the way?" Tess had confessed to her several weeks ago that Mollie seemed to be prone to dramatic mood swings. At the end of the school term, the counselor had attributed it to the usual teenage angst, because her grades hadn't suffered. Tess had thought that holding a job would give her less time to mope and watch daytime soaps.

Tess laughed. "She's improving. Then again, having a paycheck so she can buy the clothes she wants is a big morale-booster."

"Then she doesn't mind working for her mother?"

"No. I think it's giving her a new perspective. Now she understands why I'm tired at night."

"All part of growing up," Amy said cheerfully. "Our eyes do tend to open as time passes."

"Speaking of time," Tess began, "I've squeezed a few extra patients in this afternoon."

"Then you're telling me I can kiss my idea about leaving at five good-bye? My car is begging for an oil change."

"You won't be that late," Tess said. "I'm curious,

though. When are you going to trade your clunker in for a newer model?''

"What's wrong with your car?"

Once again, Ryan had seemed to float out of the woodwork to pose his question. "How do you do that?" Amy asked.

A slight wrinkle appeared on his forehead. "Do what?"

"Sneak up without us hearing you."

He shrugged. "You're just not paying attention."

*Au contraire*, she thought. She was far more aware of him than he could possibly know. Even now, her fingers tingled from wanting to touch those broad shoulders and she couldn't peel her gaze off his face. Not for the first time, her imagination teased her with what might have been if she hadn't let him close the gate.

"So what's wrong with your car?" he continued.

"Nothing. It's just old."

"About twenty years," Tess added. "Don't you think it's time she bought a new one?"

"Why?" Amy asked. "Just because the odometer turned over a hundred thousand miles? It's a Toyota and I haven't had any trouble with the way it runs. Hardly any," she corrected. "Besides, we understand each other."

"How?" he wanted to know.

She grinned. "As long as she runs, I don't let those nasty mechanics poke around her insides. She's a very modest and dignified lady."

Ryan's smile slowly widened and she felt energized for having coaxed one out of him. He left, shaking his head in obvious amusement.

"You're an absolute nut," Tess said fondly.

"Yeah, but you love me anyway."

With her spirits buoyed, Amy stayed busy for the next two hours with her patients.

At four o'clock, Mollie caught her in between rooms. At

sixteen, she was a pretty girl and showed every sign of becoming a great beauty. Her brown hair was streaked with blonde highlights, the upper curve of her ears sported an entire row of pierced earrings and everything she wore from casual jeans to dressy skirts looked good on her coltish form.

She referred back to the slip of paper in her hand. "Amy?" she asked. "A Georgia Carter called and asked if you could write a prescription for her. She said that she needs her script renewed and you know all about it."

Amy remembered the woman. She'd been under Dr Garrett's care and had come in last week for her annual check-up. At the time she hadn't been sure if her prescription was still current for another refill. Apparently the pharmacy had informed her that the time limit had elapsed.

"I'll do it right now before I get sidetracked."

Amy went to her desk and rummaged to find a prescription pad in the top drawer. "Could you pull her chart for me?"

"Sure." Mollie disappeared around the corner and returned a few minutes later with the folder.

Amy double-checked her notes from Georgia's visit and wrote the proper dosage for her antidepressant. After signing her name, she passed the slip of paper to Mollie.

"Is she going to pick it up?"

Mollie nodded. "She said she'd stop before we closed." She glanced at the drug Amy had written. "Not to be nosy, but what's this for?"

"It's an antidepressant."

"Does that mean she's, like, always unhappy?"

Amy smiled. "It's not that simple. Things happen and she becomes so overwhelmed that she can't deal with them."

Mollie appeared to consider this. "Who doesn't at times?"

"True," Amy agreed. "But Georgia gets weighed down by events and then she can't function normally."

"What do you mean?"

"Oh, like not being able to make herself get out of bed so she can hold down a job."

"Wow."

"Making a diagnosis of clinical depression is fairly complicated, so don't assume everyone who's going through a bad spell needs medication. Everyone's spirits feel low at times." Amy handed her the folder. "Would you file this for me?"

Her request reminded her of the other records she wanted to hunt down. "By the way, I looked for a few charts earlier this afternoon and couldn't find them. One was for a Jason Wentworth."

"He was in a few days ago, wasn't he?"

"Yes, he was. His mom called this afternoon for a follow-up and I couldn't find his record."

"I'm sure I filed it." Mollie tapped her forehead and narrowed her eyes in obvious thought. "I know I did."

"If you happen to run across the chart, would you, please, lay it on my desk?"

"Will do." Mollie turned away, then stopped short as she snapped her fingers. "Did you check Dr Gregory's office?"

"No," Amy said slowly. The idea hadn't occurred to her. "I don't see how it would have gotten in his office. Jason isn't his patient."

Mollie shrugged. "Sometimes he asks for charts to review before I file them. In fact, I'm almost sure he took the Wentworth folder."

Surprise, hurt, then anger filled her. After all this time, she thought she'd been making headway and he had finally started to look at her as an asset. She couldn't have been more wrong. He'd simply changed tactics. Instead of being blatantly obvious, he'd resorted to watching her covertly.

She felt manipulated, as if he'd purposely given her a false sense of security so she would relax her guard and he could catch her in some slip. The situation was too upsetting for her to ignore any more. If he was trying to discover her breaking point, he'd found it.

Turning on one heel, she marched down the hallway. The time to clear the air had come; she couldn't wait any longer.

Amy met Ryan as he left a patient. "We need to talk," she said without preamble.

He must have sensed something or seen the anger in her eyes because he didn't argue. "My office?"

"Yes." What she wanted to say was best delivered in private. She led the way and took a defensive position near the window while he stood near the door.

"You're upset."

She crossed her arms. "Your powers of observation are astounding, Doctor. I'd like to know why my patient records are ending up on *your* desk. Does the name Jason Wentworth ring any bells?"

Ryan strode toward his desk and flipped through a stack before he pulled one from the middle. "Yes, it does."

"And why do *you* have it?" she pressed on. "Checking up on my diagnosis and treatment?"

"I like to think of it as a quality assurance check."

"Quality assurance?" she repeated.

"You know. Medical facilities perform QA checks all the time to ensure the best delivery of care."

"I know what QA is all about. I just thought we were past that."

"Monitoring quality isn't something we do once and then forget," he pointed out.

"Did you pull the files for Richman, Heath and Larson, too?"

"Yes."

She didn't mind having her cases included in a QA monitor. Those were arbitrarily selected, which was the best way to discover problems. However, having her cases chosen for a random review was very different from having them chosen on purpose. "You don't trust me to do my job properly, do you?"

"I didn't at first," he admitted.

She narrowed her eyes. "Then you do now?"

Ryan perched on the edge of his desk. "Let's just say that my confidence is growing."

"But you're not truly satisfied."

"It takes time to learn each other's strengths and weaknesses." His calm tone infuriated her.

"How much time?" Warming to her subject, she waved her arms. "What hoops do I have to jump through before you finally stamp me 'approved'?"

"I don't understand why you're so upset," he said evenly. "So I've reviewed four patients in two weeks. Considering the number of people you see, that's less than one per cent."

"I'm simply not accustomed to being doubted," she said stiffly.

"Given your track record, I'm being overly generous."

"My track record?" She took a step forward. "What do you mean?"

He folded his arms across his chest and she refused to dwell on how his coat stretched across his muscles. "According to your CV, you don't stick with anything for long. You dropped out of medical school before you finished the first year. After nurse's training—"

"I know my history," she interrupted, well aware of how many jobs she'd held before she'd become a nurse-practitioner. "It took me a while to find my niche. Medical school wasn't for me."

"You still haven't worked at one place for more than twelve months."

"Dr Garrett chose to retire once his wife was diagnosed with cancer. You can't fault me because he closed his practice."

"No," he admitted. "And you can't fault me for wondering how long you'll stay here at the clinic."

His argument sounded remarkably similar to one she'd heard from her ex-boyfriend. He, too, had questioned her ability to settle down, and had decided that he wanted someone he could count on in his life—someone staid and predictable.

She'd been disappointed by their parting, but not devastated. To her, it was a telling fact of how their relationship had lacked the special spark she wanted.

Her stepsister Marta and sister Rachel had agreed. They'd sympathized over her breakup, but had admitted it hadn't been unexpected. According to them, Amy was too footloose to be tied down.

In some respects, they were right. Amy had always been searching for something but had never seemed to find whatever it was. After deciding that she couldn't float through life like pollen, she'd searched for a place to sink roots and had found it in Maple Corners. Until she'd encountered Ryan Gregory, living here had met all of her professional and personal expectations.

Now she wasn't as certain. However, she was stubborn enough not to let one man chase her away. She was through with running when the going got rough.

"I'm not leaving," she stated unequivocally.

"You won't get bored and look for greener pastures in a few months?"

"No, I won't. Can you say the same?"

"Absolutely."

She tossed him a smug glance. "I rest my case. Besides,

if I choose to go elsewhere, and that's a big *if*, my decision has no bearing on the quality of my work.''

He stretched to his full height. ''It might. People often resign after they can't crawl out of the hole they've dug for themselves.''

She moved into a near nose-to-nose position. ''I'm not digging any of your proverbial holes. Just so you'll know, when you're celebrating your retirement, I'll serve the cake and hand over your gold watch.''

A small smile tugged at his mouth. ''I certainly hope so.''

# CHAPTER SIX

STILL fuming by the time she got home, Amy took Mindy to the park in the hope of working off her frustration. She didn't have the patience this evening to putter in her flower beds or mow her grass. She wanted something physical, something so challenging it required all her concentration. Swimming a few hundred laps in Jodie's pool sounded perfect, but she didn't want to be within seeing or hearing distance of Ryan Gregory.

Jogging helped for a while, but it didn't take long for the heat and the agony of her muscles to bring that activity to a halt. In the end she resorted to her usual pastime of playing fetch, which suited Mindy just fine.

Amy heaved the newspaper roll, inwardly railing at the capricious turn her life had taken. What more could she do to prove herself or show her dedication? Nothing came to mind.

Mindy returned the paper and Amy threw it again.

She'd been furious with Ryan after she'd stormed from his office. If Tess or Dora had noticed how she hadn't been her usual bubbly self after those fifteen minutes, neither had commented. They'd probably been afraid to say a word, she thought wryly.

Thank goodness her last few cases had been simple. No doubt these patient files would end up on Ryan's desk for one of his infamous reviews. All but certain he would later accuse her of letting her emotions interfere with her professional abilities if she so much as didn't cross every t and dot every i, she'd made a point of documenting each detail, no matter how insignificant it had been.

Watching Mindy take off like a streak of lightning with a doggy smile on her face, she wished her life could be as simple. Food, plenty of love and exercise were all that it took to make her pet happy. Mindy certainly had nothing to prove.

Of course, not every dog was as spoiled as hers. Those who were mistreated often developed bad habits or turned downright mean. Her scenario didn't fit Ryan—he wouldn't be as caring a physician as he was—but something had turned him into a skeptical person where she was concerned.

Yes, she knew about his bad experiences with his former nurse-practitioners, but she hated being judged for someone else's actions. There were levels of competence in all professions and lumping everyone in the same category was both foolish and totally unrealistic.

By the same token, not every physician she'd worked with graduated at the top of his class. She wasn't about to swear off all of them because a few had squeaked by and their skills showed it. He wouldn't appreciate being labeled a quack because a person had had a bad experience with one of his colleagues. He had a right to be distrusted for his own mistakes, not someone else's, and he owed her the same courtesy.

If she'd taken time to prepare her defense before she'd rushed into his office, she could have argued her case more effectively. Right now, though, she was far too irritated at him to bring up the subject again. If and when she did, she wanted to sound as cooly professional as possible.

An hour passed. Perspiration trickled down her face and between her breasts. Her right arm and shoulder ached from over-exertion and she was finally ready to go home. A leisurely dip in Jodie's pool sounded like pure heaven.

With most of her anger gone, she could view the situation more objectively. Clearly, nothing she said would change Ryan's attitude. He was a man who put his faith in actions, not words, so her only option was to continue with what she'd done before—practice the best medicine she possibly could. As someone who liked to move in and "fix" problems, her decision seemed rather impassive and apathetic, but she had no choice.

She hadn't totally *accepted* her lot, but at least she'd reached a point of resignation. She could walk into the clinic tomorrow and not be tempted to booby-trap his office with buckets of water and shoe polish. Pushing herself to her physical limits had burned off her anger.

Mindy dropped the roll near her feet and wagged her tail.

"All right." She capitulated under the full force of the spaniel's clear-eyed gaze. "Once more for good measure before we head for home."

Mindy panted and danced away a few yards. "Keep going," Amy encouraged. Finally, when the spaniel had what Amy considered a good start, she heaved the teeth-marked roll as far as she could.

The moment it left her hand she knew she'd lost control of her throwing arm. Mindy's toy flew dangerously close to the paved jogging path as it curved into a stand of trees along the edge of the field.

Mindy jumped to catch the paper in her mouth and, while Amy watched in horror, collided with a jogger who'd just rounded the bend. With a loud exclamation from the unsuspecting victim and a high-pitched squeal from Mindy, the two crashed to the ground.

Amy ran forward while the dog scrambled to her feet and stood shaking beside the man who lay across the track. "Oh, my goodness," she cried, dropping to kneel in the grass beside his head. "I'm so sorry."

Recognizing Ryan, her dismay intensified and formed a knot in the pit of her stomach. "Where are you hurt?" she asked. Guided by her instincts, she automatically ran her hands along his bare legs and arms to check for obvious breaks.

"I'm OK," he said sounding dazed. "Just battered and bruised."

Relief eased the lump of worry. "Lie there until you get your breath back," she ordered.

He closed his eyes. "What happened?"

Instantly thinking of concussion, she checked his scalp. It was far too tempting to concentrate on the texture of his hair as she ran her fingers through the strands, but she didn't. "You and Mindy collided as we were playing fetch. I don't feel any knots or see any cuts. You have a hard head." *In more ways than one*, she finished silently.

"Lucky me," he said wryly.

"How does your neck feel?"

He tested it. "Stiff."

"And the rest of you? I didn't notice any breaks." She noticed a host of other things—athletic shorts that molded his hips, a top that revealed broad shoulders and a light covering of hair on his chest, and a long expanse of muscular thighs—that didn't pertain to medicine.

Ryan moved his arms and legs. "Sore, but I'll live."

She sat back on her heels, flooded with an immeasurable sense of relief. "Good. No real harm done, then." He might have aggravated her, but causing bodily injury had never entered her mind. In her wildest dreams, she'd never imagined that a runner would appear on that path at the exact instant she threw the paper, much less that *he* would be the runner.

After their heated conversation, however, he might disagree.

"Can you sit up?" At his nod, she lent him a hand.

His face turned slightly green. "Are you dizzy?"

"A little." He bent one leg and left the other outstretched across the track. "With the acres of unobstructed lawn here, I can't believe you chose to play fetch near the track."

Although he didn't mention the word "irresponsible" she heard it loud and clear in his dry tone and saw it in his eyes.

"My arm was tired," she defended herself, not going into the reasons why. "It was an accident."

"I'll say." He accepted her outstretched hand, but before she could pull him to his feet an odd rumbling noise grew louder, seeming to come from behind.

Unable to initially identify the sound, Amy glanced around to find the source. By the time she realized what it was, a youth whizzed around the corner on his scooter in a blur.

With Ryan's back to the boy, Amy had only a split second's notice to yank him off the path to safety.

It wasn't enough.

This time, Amy lay underneath Ryan and the boy had fallen in the opposite direction. His scooter rested on its side only a few inches from Ryan's foot. Mindy ran around the scene, barking furiously as if wanting to participate in whatever game the humans were playing.

Amy dragged in a breath that was filled with the scent of green grass and male sweat. "I didn't do it," she said inanely, certain he'd blame her for this, too.

His muttered curses drifted through the evening air.

"Hey, mister. Are you all right?" The boy's eyes were huge as he leaned over them, effectively blocking the sun from Amy's face.

"No, I'm not," he snapped.

"What's wrong?" Amy asked. "If you'll roll off me, I can—"

"I can't roll off you." He sounded pained. "I can't move my leg."

Amy muttered an expletive of her own. "OK," she said calmly. "Give me a second and I'll just wiggle out." While Ryan did what he could by raising his torso up while he leaned on one elbow, she slithered free.

"How are you?" she asked the young teenager, who wore a bicycle helmet, wrist-, elbow- and knee-pads.

"I'm fine." He grinned. "Guess my gear came in handy." He glanced at Ryan who now sported a sheen of perspiration on his forehead and upper lip. "Looks like he should have been wearing some, too."

Ryan glared at Amy. "Don't I know it."

Amy quickly turned her attention to her patient. "Which one is…?" She didn't finish her sentence. His injuries were obvious. It wasn't his leg, but his ankle. In one spot, the skin bulged outward from the broken bone and his left foot stuck out at an unnatural angle.

"Oh, my," she mumbled, certain he would need an orthopedic surgeon to repair the damage.

Ryan struggled to raise himself on his elbows. "How bad is it?"

"Golly, mister. Your foot looks like it's gonna fall off."

"Let me see," Ryan demanded.

Amy placed a hand on his chest to push him down. "Your ankle's broken."

"I can feel it," he snapped. "How bad?" he repeated.

"You won't be jogging for a while," she replied.

"Damn." He flung an arm over his eyes.

The distinctive sound of moving metal parts and wheels rolling against the asphalt came next. "Good news," the boy said in a relief-filled voice. "My scooter's not broken."

"At least something came out of this unscathed."

Ryan's sarcasm clearly went over the boy's head. Amy, however, bit back a smile. The situation was far from funny, but if she didn't find some humor in it, she'd burst into tears. She might not have actually hurt Ryan, but she'd certainly contributed to his injuries.

"My brother broke his ankle last summer," the teenager supplied. "It took him a year before he could play basketball again."

"Guess it's a good thing I don't play basketball," Ryan said dryly.

At least he wasn't yelling and screaming, Amy thought.

"What's your name, kid?" Ryan asked, lowering his arm to look him in the eye.

Fear crossed the youth's face. "Are you gonna sue me, mister?"

"No, he's not going to sue you," Amy interjected. "It was an accident. Now, what's your name?"

He hesitated. "Luke. Luke Wagner."

Ryan grimaced. "Well, Luke, I'm afraid you're going to have to go for help."

Amy stared at Ryan. "Don't you have a cellphone?"

"Not on me," he said.

"Mister—"

She ignored Luke. "I can't believe you don't carry one at all times."

"I can't believe I'm lying in the park with a broken ankle," he groused. "So we're even."

"Ma'am—" Luke began.

Once again, Amy didn't give the boy time to interrupt her conversation. "How are people supposed to get in touch with you in an emergency?"

"I'm not on call tonight," he said smugly. "Contrary to what you may think, I don't work *all* the time. And speaking of cellphones, where's yours?"

"In my car. In front of my house."

He rolled his eyes. "OK, kid. Er, Luke. You're going to have to climb on your scooter and find a telephone."

"Why?" Luke asked, clearly puzzled. "I can call from

here. That's what I've been trying to tell you.'' He reached into the back pocket of his denim shorts and whipped out a cellphone. A few punches of the buttons later, he was giving their location to someone on the other end.

Ryan exchanged a glance with Amy, his disgust obvious. ''It's pretty sad when a thirteen-year-old kid carries more high-tech gadgets and is more prepared than we are.''

''I've certainly learned my lesson,'' she said fervently.

Luke clicked the phone closed. ''An ambulance is on its way,'' he revealed importantly. He leaned over Ryan's leg. ''Shouldn't we splint it? I have a rag in my pocket and I'll bet I can find a few sticks.''

''No.'' Amy and Ryan spoke simultaneously.

''If we were going to move him,'' Amy said kindly, ''then we definitely would want to stabilize his foot. But since an ambulance is on its way, we'll let the emergency medical team do the honors. They'll probably give him a painkiller beforehand.''

''You'd better believe they will,'' Ryan muttered.

Amy blotted his face with the edge of her shirt. ''I feel awful about this.''

''Me, too, mister,'' Luke chimed in.

He acknowledged their sympathy with a brief nod. ''It could have been worse, I suppose. All three of us could be sprawled across the grass with broken bones.''

A siren's wail suddenly seemed to make the few people in the park take notice. As the emergency medical crew approached the path, interested bystanders slowly began to congregate in the vicinity. Amy attached Mindy's leash and gave her into Luke's care so she wouldn't become a nuisance.

Amy briefed the two technicians on Ryan's condition and before long he was carried across the field and loaded in the back of the ambulance.

"I'll be along as soon as I take Mindy home," she told him.

"You don't need to—" he began.

"Yes, I do," Amy said firmly.

The ambulance left, its lights flashing. After memorizing Luke's phone number in case Ryan would like to speak to his parents, she sent him on his way. Then she rushed to her house, settled Mindy in the backyard and showered in record time. Less than ten minutes later, she was laying rubber on the asphalt in her hurry to reach the hospital.

"How's Dr Gregory?" she asked the ER nurse. "I'm his nurse-practitioner," she added in case the woman questioned her.

"He's in X-ray. If you want to wait in trauma one, he'll be back soon."

"Did you call Dr Feldman?" Not only did he have an excellent reputation but, as the town's only orthopedic surgeon, his services were in great demand.

"He's in surgery and will stop by as soon as he's finished."

Unable to sit, Amy paced the floor inside the small area until she was sure she'd worn the flecked design completely off the tile. Finally, voices and a familiar whisper of wheels announced his arrival moments before two nurses rolled Ryan's bed into the room.

He lay prone, with his feet slightly elevated, and seemed surprised to see her. "You came."

"I said I would."

"I thought you might change your mind."

She shrugged, hiding how much his skepticism bothered her. "My stepmom always told us to do what we say and say what we mean."

"Wise words to live by," he said. "Provided that one *can* live up to them."

"It's not so hard," she said lightly.

"Is that why you came? Just because you said you would?" He sounded curious, as if he wanted to understand her motives.

"You're new in town and I didn't think you should be alone." That much was true. However, she also had a healthy measure of guilt to contend with, and she really was concerned about him. Not wanting to answer more questions on the subject, she asked, "What's the radiologist's verdict?"

"It's broken," he said.

Amy stared at him with exasperation. "Tell me what I don't know."

"From looking at the X-rays and the amount of hardware Feldman will have to use, I'll probably set off alarms the next time I walk through an airport's security checkpoint."

Before she could reply, Dr Feldman sauntered in with the films in hand, still dressed in surgical garb. A man in his early fifties, Feldman peered over his reading glasses to compare Ryan's uncovered foot to the radiology pictures.

"Excellent diagnosis. You should have gone into orthopedics," he said. "You're definitely a candidate for a few screws and possibly a plate. Distal pulse is good, so at least we don't have to worry about vascular injury. How's the pain?"

Ryan grimaced. "Not too bad."

"When did you eat last?" Feldman asked.

"Lunchtime."

"I could operate tonight, but I've already got someone ahead of you. How about if we fix you up first thing in the morning?"

"Fine."

"Run over by a scooter, hey?" Feldman grinned.

"A freak accident. It started with a dog, but I won't bore you with the details."

Feldman guffawed. "Something tells me this story is

anything but boring. Just relax and I'll see you tomorrow. Any questions?''

''When can I go back to work?''

Feldman thought aloud. ''Today is what, Wednesday? I'd say next Monday. Friday might be pushing things a bit.''

''Monday will work.''

''You may not be able to stand for long periods of time,'' Feldman warned. ''Maneuvering crutches and being in a cast will slow you down.''

''I'll manage.''

Feldman sent an enquiring glance in Amy's direction as if he expected her to be Ryan's voice of reason. ''We'll work something out,'' she told him.

''You bet we will,'' Ryan muttered.

Feldman laughed. ''Spoken like a man who thinks he's indispensable. Don't expect to function at your usual one hundred and ten per cent. Give yourself time to recover.'' He grinned. ''Now I'm off to put another Humpty Dumpty back together.''

Feldman left, smiling at his own joke. Ryan didn't appear amused as he leaned his head against the pillows. ''Humpty Dumpty, my eye.''

''You wanted a good orthopedic man, not a comedian.'' She changed the subject. ''Is there anyone you want to call? Family? Friend? A special someone?''

Ryan raised an eyebrow. ''For a one-day surgery procedure? No.''

''I just thought someone might be interested in what had happened to you.''

''Are you asking about a significant other?''

She was, but she didn't want to admit it. ''Just trying to be helpful.''

''Thanks, but there isn't anyone I want you to call. My parents are divorced. If one of them came, the other would feel obligated, and they don't get along well. I'd rather not deal with that right now."

"That's too bad," she said sympathetically. "My step-sister Marta and my sister Rachel would be upset if I didn't tell them I was in the hospital for any reason. They practically raised me after my stepmom died."

"Where was your father?"

"He was around physically, but never in spirit. I guess losing two wives was more than he could handle and he died several years later. Anyway, I think of Marta as more a full sister than a stepsister. I'll have to tell you about how Rachel and I got Marta and her grandfather back together." She smiled at the memory. "Enough about me. Are you sure there isn't someone you'd like to hold your hand?"

"I'm positive."

The idea that Ryan would see himself alone through this made her all the more determined that he wouldn't. After all, she had to do something to assuage her guilt. "Then you won't mind if I stick around and make sure Feldman doesn't operate on the wrong ankle?"

He groaned. "Another joker." Yet a half smile crossed his mouth. Amy wasn't sure if her gentle teasing had coaxed at his smile or if he was relieved to have company.

Later, after he'd been transferred to a room on the surgical floor and he'd fallen asleep during the TV evening news, she drew the blanket over his shoulders. He looked so peaceful, so *boyish* as he lay against the white sheets that she couldn't resist brushing a soft good-night kiss on his mouth. How her feelings for him had changed in the space of a few short hours.

Amy returned early the next morning with a few personal items and the change of clothes he'd requested while the staff hurried to complete his pre-op blood tests, IVs and paperwork. She'd barely had time to confess to notifying Dr Hyde before the older physician arrived.

"Mind if I scrub in?" he asked. "I have to protect my investment, you know."

Ryan smiled. "The more the merrier. Did Feldman call you?"

"I did," Amy interjected. "I thought *someone* at the clinic should know why you weren't at work today."

"I would have been upset if you hadn't," Dr Hyde declared. "Do you have a way home this afternoon?"

Amy spoke up before Ryan could answer. "I'll take him after the office closes."

"Good enough." Satisfied that this detail had been taken care of, Phillip turned to Amy. "I'll let you know how things go inside."

"Please, do." Alone with Ryan once again, she noticed the tension he'd been trying to hide from his partner. For a man who liked to oversee little details, he undoubtedly was finding it difficult to let go and put his faith in someone else's hands. The realization made her feel better to a small degree. His distrust wasn't directed solely toward her.

"You don't have to act as my taxi service, you know."

"I know. I want to. Because you live in my backyard—" she grinned "—I'm the most logical person, so don't argue."

"Would it do any good if I did?"

"Absolutely none." She changed the subject. "You've never had surgery before?"

"No."

"The idea can be pretty frightening," she admitted. "As a kid, I was in and out of the hospital a lot. I was the adventuresome one of the family."

"I figured you were."

"Really? How did you guess? Anyway, I had a lot of broken bones from falling out of trees, jumping off swings and trying to do stunts on my bike."

"A regular daredevil."

She grinned. "No, I just wanted to try something different. Anyway, the point I'm trying to make is that our fear of the unknown is worse than the actual procedure."

"I *know* what's going to happen, Amy. I'm a doctor, remember?"

Oddly enough, he appeared somewhat vulnerable in his white hospital gown. "You know the steps," she corrected, "but it's different when you're the patient. As medical people, sometimes we know too much."

"Yeah."

She clutched his hand. "You're going to sail through surgery. Wait and see. And when Feldman is done, I'll be here to give you a blow-by-blow account."

"Promise?"

This was a test—she knew it as well as she knew her own name. It was also a test that she didn't intend to fail.

"Cross my heart."

A minute later, the surgery personnel arrived to take him away and she was left with the hardest job of all. Waiting.


"You're late."

Amy re-entered Ryan's hospital room after five p.m. and smiled at the way his greeting matched the impatience on his face. "I was driving on fumes, and since you aren't in any shape to push my car home I stopped at the filling station first."

"You could have called."

"Yes, I could have," she responded patiently to his petulance, "but I didn't think it necessary to explain a five-minute delay."

"Fifteen," he corrected.

He'd obviously been watching the clock closely. "Did you think I wasn't coming or are you that anxious to give up all this pampering?" She motioned around the room.

"Pampering? You've got to be joking."

"Come, now. Your meals are brought to you and everything you could possibly want is at your beck and call. By the way, I've heard the single nurses drew straws to see who got to take care of you. You know what they say about patients falling in love with their nurses."

A flush spread upward from his neck. "Mick was on duty so everyone's hearts are still intact."

Revealing the male nurse's sexual preference would, no doubt, have sent Ryan into orbit. The news was best saved for a time when Ryan's disposition wasn't so stressed and when Mick wasn't within hearing distance. She tried to refocus the conversation.

"Actually, as grumpy as you are, I think the staff will throw a party once you're discharged. It's been proven how doctors make the worst patients."

"Very funny."

"Seriously, though, I don't know why you're in such a rush to go home to your empty house. At least here you'll have—"

"Someone coming into my room every five minutes to check my temperature or ask if I need more painkillers."

"They're just providing good quality care," she pointed out.

He crossed his arms. "What do you call it when they even volunteer to help me change clothes?"

Having seen him in everything from athletic apparel to wet shorts that left little to the imagination, she could easily understand why the single nurses would vie for the task. "A perk of the job?" she teased.

"You're a regular clown today, aren't you?"

She grinned. "Sunny had the honor."

"I know. She dropped by this afternoon. At first I thought it was you, but then I realized it wasn't."

"Really? How could you tell us apart?"

"You smell different."

"I probably shouldn't ask, but is that 'different' as in good or bad?"

He shrugged. "It depends on if you like the smell of a doctor's office or not."

She would have preferred it if he'd waxed poetic over how she reminded him of spring flowers or the air after rain, but *a doctor's office*? She was clearly paying far too much for her tiny bottle of designer scent if he couldn't notice it over the odor of alcohol and disinfectant.

"Remind me to put perfume on my Christmas list," she said dryly. Then, before he could tell her something else that she didn't want to hear, she diverted the subject back to him. "How's the ankle?"

"It aches."

"Are you keeping it elevated?"

He gave her an exasperated look. "Does it look like I can do anything else?"

"Sorry," she said, unrepentant. "Have you had any rest?"

"How does anyone rest in hospital? I've been poked and prodded to death. If there's a staff shortage, I certainly can't tell. They've all been in my room at one time or another."

She smiled at his exaggeration. Before she could say anything, he continued.

"In between, I've watched television, listened to the noise in the hallway and waited for you to spring me from this joint."

She didn't fault him for being crabby. Most people complained about having to go home to get any rest. "You should be enjoying the attention."

"You can have the attention. I want peace and quiet."

"Then peace and quiet it is. Are you all packed and ready?" She glanced around and found the duffel bag she'd brought from his home on a wheeled cart in the corner.

"Since three," he stated.

"What about the paperwork?"

"I've already signed everything in triplicate."

Amy eyed an arrangement of daisies and two potted plants on the counter-top. While he'd been in surgery, a steady parade of volunteers had filled the room with blooms of all kinds. "What happened to the rest of your flowers?"

"Dora came by and is taking them to the nursing home for me. I'm keeping these."

She wondered why he'd chosen daisies when he'd had an entire plant kingdom at his disposal. The yellow and white daisies in a ceramic work boot seemed too whimsical for a man who didn't have a whimsical bone in his entire body. "Good choice. Daisies are my favorite, too."

He grunted and she didn't know if he was pleased or unhappy by her comment. "Can we go?"

Aware that his curt tone had nothing to do with her and everything to do with his eagerness to leave, she simply smiled and gathered his things together.

Mick arrived and wheeled him to the elevator for a quick trip downstairs to her car parked near the "Patient Loading" sign. Luckily, that portion of the curb was situated under a covering which provided some protection from the weather. Although the temperature was well into the nineties, the shade and her open windows had kept her car from becoming a veritable sauna.

As soon as Mick had installed Ryan in the back seat so he could stretch out his leg, she drove off with her air-conditioner on full blast, conscious of Ryan resting his head against the door and sighing before he closed his eyes.

"Are you in pain?"

"No. Appreciating the freedom."

Amy laughed. "You weren't in prison, you know."

"It sure felt like it. I couldn't move a muscle without someone looking over my shoulder."

What poetic justice, she thought. "Just because you're

at home, it doesn't mean it won't still happen,'' she warned.
''I gave Feldman my word that I wouldn't let you overtax
yourself and I can be pretty formidable when necessary.''

''I'll keep it in mind,'' he said dryly.

In less than thirty minutes, with the help of the crutches
she'd removed from her trunk, he was resting on his living
room sofa with his leg stretched out on the ottoman while
she toted in his duffel bag and the plants.

Without a word, she adjusted the temperature setting on
his air conditioner and placed the evening newspaper, a
bottle of cold water and a flat box on the coffee table within
reach.

''In honor of your homecoming, I brought you a little
something to sweeten your disposition. Have one.''

His eyes lit up and he ripped into the box of chocolate-
covered caramels. ''How did you know I love these?''

''I saw an empty box in your trash can the other day.
Enjoy.''

''I will.''

Obviously, the sugar and his surroundings did their work
because the lines on his face became less pronounced as
he relaxed against the cushions.

''Is there anything else you'd like me to do or get for
you?''

Ryan wondered what she'd do if he explained what he
*really* wanted…and it had nothing to do with fetching him
a drink, a newspaper or his slippers. All day long, while
he'd waited for his pain medication to kick in, he'd passed
the time reliving their kiss. Granted, it hadn't been the wis-
est thing to do because the memory gave him a pain of a
different sort, but at least it had taken his mind off his
throbbing ankle.

He'd also recalled bits and pieces of when they'd lain
entangled in the park, but to his great regret his injury had
made most of that particular incident vague.

Because all of those options were out of the question—at least right now—he'd ask for the next best thing.

"Tell me how things went at the office this afternoon."

"Dr Feldman said—"

Ryan crossed his arms. "I know what he said. I was there when he told me to take things easy. *You*, however, promised that you'd update me once I got home." He glanced around the room. "Here I am."

She appeared resigned, which was good because if she refused he didn't have a whole lot of options. If she walked out, she could be halfway across town before he hobbled out of the house. On the other hand, she only lived a few yards away. He wasn't proficient with steps yet but, hey, he had all the time in the world.

"It was busy," she admitted, sitting next to him on the sofa. Ryan privately patted himself on the back for his lack of furniture.

"Tess called everyone with an appointment and gave them a choice of rescheduling for next week or coming in and I'd see them. About half decided to wait."

"And the other half?" He raised an eyebrow.

"I worked them in between my cases."

"Anything I should know about?"

"Almost everything was straightforward. A sinus infection, an earache, an ingrown toenail and a case of poison ivy."

"You said 'almost' everything," he said, picking up on her qualifier. "What wasn't?"

"I had a woman in her forties who'd noticed a painless nodule at the base of her throat."

"Thyroid?"

"I'm guessing that it is. I ordered the usual blood tests along with a full battery of thyroid hormones. We should have the reports by the beginning of next week."

"Any other symptoms?"

"Fatigue, but she doesn't know if it's due to being extra busy this summer or not."

"She'll need a fine-needle aspiration biopsy."

"I thought so, but that's beyond my expertise."

He thought for a moment. "Malignancies in other parts of the body can involve the thyroid. Melanoma, lymphoma, breast cancer..."

"Which is why I wanted to discuss her case with you. Do you want me to send her to Dr Jackson tomorrow or shall I make an appointment with Dr Perry, the surgeon, for the biopsy?"

"I'll see her on Monday."

"I hope you're not planning a full day," she cautioned.

"I'll come in the morning and see how I manage," he compromised. "I can give her a complete physical before she sees Perry in the afternoon."

Deep in his plans, he didn't pay her any attention until he glanced at her and noticed a thoughtful expression on her face. "What's wrong now?"

"Something just occurred to me," she said slowly. "You don't trust your colleagues either, do you?"

She'd hit remarkably close to home. "This isn't about trust. This is about taking care of my responsibilities."

"You can't work twenty-four seven for the rest of your life."

"I realize that."

"Then why won't you let Dr Jackson examine Mrs Obermeyer? Or Dr Perry for that matter?"

He had a feeling she wouldn't let the subject rest. "Because, in my last practice, one of my colleagues misdiagnosed a patient of mine. The boy nearly died."

# CHAPTER SEVEN

AMY had suspected that Ryan's distrust was rooted in something catastrophic and now he'd confirmed her hunch. "What happened?"

"It's all rather convoluted and not very pretty," he warned her.

"Things like that usually aren't." She softened her voice. "I have all night, so take your time."

He reached for the bottle of water as if to delay this unhappy walk down memory lane.

"My first nurse-practitioner was so unsure of herself she ran to me with every little thing. My NP at the next place I went to was a woman who oozed confidence. Everyone in the office spoke highly of her and I immediately gave her free rein.

"Eventually, I took a vacation and went skiing for a week with some friends. I'd made arrangements with my partner to handle any cases that my NP couldn't, and left for New Mexico, believing I'd left my patients in good hands.

"While I was gone, a woman brought in her teenage son with abdominal pain. He'd been in numerous times, and we'd never found anything conclusive in his blood work or sonograms. After several hours, the pain would go away as quickly as it had come."

Grimacing, he shifted positions. Without asking, Amy took a throw pillow from the sofa and slipped it under his cast.

"When he showed up in my NP's office on the Friday, she assumed it was another verse of the same song, and decided not to order any testing. She basically told his mother to go home, give him two aspirin and come back on Monday. By late afternoon he was worse and the mother brought him back, insisting on seeing a physician."

"Did she send him to your partner?"

He nodded. "He ordered another CBC. The white-cell count was a little higher than his previous one, but because he was running behind schedule and because of the history my NP gave him, he decided not to pursue it. In the meantime, she prescribed a laxative and conveniently ignored his rising temperature."

Amy frowned. An elevated temp wasn't something one dismissed. "How could she do that?"

He shrugged. "She had plans for that evening and didn't want to cancel them."

"Why, that's horrible!"

"Around midnight, the boy's family brought him to the ER. By two o'clock, he was in surgery."

"What did they find?" she asked, already suspecting his answer.

"His appendix ruptured just as the surgeon began to remove it. The teenager pulled through, thanks to all the antibiotics thrown at him, but he was in the hospital for a long time."

"And you blame yourself."

"More or less. My patients trusted me to find adequate coverage while I was gone."

"But you did."

He shook his head and took a long drag of his water. "No, I didn't. I starting digging as soon as I got back to town. I felt like a real idiot once I discovered my NP's tendency to take short cuts whenever her work conflicted with her lifestyle."

No wonder he was so leery of her. Not only had their

first meeting been while she'd been dressed in a clown suit, but she'd rearranged her schedule in order to act the part.

"And the doctor?" she asked.

"This wasn't the first time my illustrious partner had taken half-measures when asked to cover for another physician. I'd never realized why he rarely filled in for anyone, but after that episode I had my suspicions. Had I not accepted both of them on faith, I might have saved that boy, his family and myself some grief."

"Yes, but—"

"After the incident, I questioned if I wanted to remain in his practice if I couldn't trust him. Things came to a head a month later when he reneged on our contract. I then understood why he'd brought in so many physicians over the years."

"So you came to Maple Corners."

Ryan nodded. "I hated to leave my patients, but because of a clause in the fine print I couldn't set up my own office in the area. The woman I was dating refused to understand why I didn't 'go with the flow', in her words, so we broke up. Phillip's offer came as a godsend, and I learned a valuable lesson."

Which wasn't to trust anyone, she thought.

"I'm sorry for what happened," Amy said slowly, hoping to encourage him to not let this incident rule his life. "But with your ankle the way it is, you're going to have to trust us to handle our jobs. You can't do everything yourself."

He let out a long, resigned breath, but didn't answer.

"I understand your reason for being so cautious, but we've worked together for about a month, right?" He nodded and she continued. "You've seen me with my patients, checked my charts and, for all I know, installed a hidden camera."

He grinned at this remark, which she took as a good sign.

"And at any time, did you find fault with anything I've done?"

He paused. "No," he said slowly.

"Then can you trust me to take good care of the people who come to us?"

Once again, he hesitated. "More or less."

As a vote of confidence, his response lacked resounding enthusiasm, but at least he hadn't totally denied her. "I won't let you down."

"Don't make promises you can't keep."

"I never have," she said evenly. "Nor do I intend to start now."

Something unreadable flickered in his gaze, but she didn't flinch. Suddenly, a wary acceptance crossed his features. "Fair enough."

Her pager took that moment to go off and she read the number on the display. "May I use your phone? Mine is in my car."

"Help yourself." Ryan noticed she didn't have any difficulty in finding her way to the kitchen where it was located.

Her low voice as she spoke to the person who'd called her reminded him of warm honey. For all his fuss about wanting to be alone, he wanted Amy to be with him. Having her nearby was better than a pain pill. Her wit and her smile made everything else fade into insignificance and he hoped she wouldn't have to leave.

A second later, she reappeared beside the sofa. "I have to go. Is there anything you need?"

"A pillow," he said promptly. "There's one in my bedroom. First door—"

"On the right," she finished, her voice fading as she headed down the hall.

Ordinarily, having someone know his house as well as she obviously did would have bothered him immensely. It was different with Amy. Somehow, she fitted in as if she belonged.

She returned, carrying two pillows. "Lean forward."

He complied, his nose coming too close to her breasts for comfort. She smelled of flowers, sunshine and pure woman, and he hardly noticed what she was doing behind his back.

"How's that?" she asked, pushing him gently against the cushions.

Her face was now close to his and he couldn't tear his gaze from her mouth. "I lied."

A wrinkle appeared between her eyebrows. "You don't want the pillows?"

"You don't smell like a doctor's office. You remind me of spring."

Her smile grew. "I'm glad to hear it." She tried to straighten, but he grabbed her upper arms to stop her. "Did you kiss me last night?"

She opened her mouth, then closed it as pink tinged her cheeks. "I thought you were asleep."

"I was dozing," he said.

"I wasn't— I mean I…"

He grinned at her discomfiture. "Would you do it again?"

Her eyes widened and began to sparkle. "Is this a rhetorical question or are you asking for a repeat performance?"

"Practice makes perfect," he said promptly.

Her eyes narrowed slightly and filled with a thoughtful gleam as she puckered her lips ever so slightly. "How much medication have you had today?"

"Considering how my ankle feels," he said dryly, "not enough."

"In that case…" She moved closer. Eager to span the distance, he leaned forward and hungrily met her mouth.

The contact was as powerful as a bolt of lightning and his cares seemed to melt into mind-numbing nothingness. His thoughts, his senses, his entire body seemed to be consumed by the woman who stood over him.

She slowly pulled away, looking as shaken as he felt. "Wow. I'd better get going or else..." The rest of her sentence went unspoken, but he knew what she meant. "I don't know what to say."

"Come back for dinner," he said. "Bring Mindy, too, if you want a chaperone."

"I may be a while," she warned.

"I can wait," he said. "I'm not hungry right now. How does eight o'clock sound?"

She beamed. "Perfect. I'll pick up a pizza on my way over."

Ryan watched her leave, feeling abandoned in spite of her promise to return. He had no reason to feel as if she'd deserted him—being called out for a patient came with the territory. Besides, he'd wanted peace and quiet. His hospital room had been as busy as a church on Easter morning and he'd waited all day for the solitude of his home.

Yet as he stared at the perky flower arrangement he'd saved out of the multitudes he'd received—including one from Luke and his parents—he remembered why he hadn't been able to give this one away. The yellow and white daisies in a ceramic shoe reminded him of Amy in her clown boots.

After the kiss they'd just shared, he was playing with fire. She wasn't the type of person who could step into his low-key lifestyle and be happy there for long. While he didn't mind attending an occasional gathering and spending time with friends, a steady diet of those affairs didn't appeal to him. The last woman he'd dated had tried to change him, but they'd both ended up miserable.

He would be foolish to let Amy tie his emotions in proverbial knots when their differences were too far apart to allow for compromise. Yet he was male enough to take her feminine companionship for as long as she offered it.

One hundred and eighteen minutes until she returned.

He hadn't been able to sleep at the hospital, but now that he was home he was more than ready to grab forty winks. Going to his bedroom required too much of an effort and he drifted off where he sat.

When he awoke, he was surprised to discover that three hours had passed. Thinking Amy might have come and gone without him noticing, he grabbed his crutches and made his way slowly into the kitchen. No pizza boxes there.

Twilight was falling, but her house remained completely dark. It wasn't unheard of to run into problems or to get a second call, but he'd hoped she would have a quiet evening.

He swung himself back to the sofa and collapsed against the cushions. This small amount of exercise proved one thing. There was simply no way he could function at work like he had before the accident. It would take every ounce of his energy to look after his own affairs, much less worry what Amy was doing down the hall. As she'd so politely pointed out, she hadn't done anything during this past month to raise any of his mental flags, so perhaps it was time to trust her to perform the job for which she'd been trained.

Amy was nothing like Miranda. Ninety per cent of him was sure of it. Fear had governed the remaining ten per cent. If it hadn't been for Luke and his scooter-from-hell, he wouldn't be in this position of changing the status quo. Fate, however, had other plans. He could only hope those plans wouldn't include another disaster. The next patient might not be as lucky.

He clicked on the television and surfed the channels, but nothing held his interest for long. The telephone provided a welcome interruption.

"Is Amy there?" Dora asked.

"No," he answered, surprised to hear from his nurse. "I'm expecting her, though. Do you want to leave a message?"

"No-o-o."

Dora's drawn-out answer didn't seem right and his instincts kicked into overdrive. "What's wrong?" he asked.

"Nothing," she answered quickly. "At least, I'm sure it's nothing."

Her tone suggested otherwise. "She's half an hour late," he said, hoping to draw information from his nurse. "I thought maybe she'd call, but she hasn't."

Dora made a noise sounding remarkably like a whimper.

"You might as well tell me what's going on," he said in his firmest voice.

"You'll find out anyway, I suppose."

"Spit it out, Dora," he said impatiently.

"Amy left a message on my machine earlier to ask if I'd go with her to visit a family on the south side of town. I couldn't because I wasn't home, so I assume she called someone else."

Although he'd only lived in Maple Corners a few weeks, he'd already been told to avoid driving in the area south of the railroad tracks after dark, for safety's sake. He hadn't given the suggestion much credence at the time, but now he couldn't force the warning out of his mind.

"She went on a house call?" He'd thought she'd gone to the hospital, not the part of town where even the pizza delivery boys refused to go after eight. Her tardiness no longer seemed a situation to be taken in his stride, but one with ominous overtones.

Worry, laced with a healthy amount of fear, filled his gut. For such a little thing, she had a tendency to charge into situations impulsively, expecting her bravado, not her brawn, to smooth the path. When she returned, he intended to give her a large piece of his mind for her foolishness.

*If* she returned.

He shook the thought out of his head. The idea of anyone hurting her was too horrifying to consider. He could only hope that she'd asked someone besides Dora to accompany her. If it hadn't been for his ankle, she might have asked him.

"I'm sure she had her reasons for going," Dora said.

"Would she have taken someone else?"

"I don't know." She paused. "Do you have a police scanner?"

He knew of many people who owned the electronic device in order to monitor law enforcement and other service personnel's radio transmissions. As a physician, emergencies usually knocked at his door so he'd never felt the need to look for them. Until now. "No."

"I don't either, but I know someone who does. I'll see what I can find out."

Ryan drew a deep breath. He wasn't one to imagine the worst, but he couldn't think of a realistic reason for why she hadn't telephoned during those three hours.

Unless she hadn't been able to call.

He wanted to hop in his car and find her, but he couldn't drive with all the painkillers in his system. Instead, he glared at his ankle and cursed scooters under his breath. "Keep me posted," he told her tersely.

Breaking the connection, he held the phone in his hand. The two of them made quite a pair. He trusted few people and Amy trusted everyone. What had she gotten herself into?

Amy knelt on the rug that covered the worn-out linoleum in the Mullens' house and unwrapped the makeshift bandage that covered ten-year-old Tony's foot from his ankle to his toes. The dark-haired boy with eyes as black as night sat stoically on the chair, his skinny little arms gripping both sides of the seat as if he were bracing himself for pain which was inevitable. From the appearance of the yellowish pus oozing from the long, deep cut across his arch and the reddish streaks radiating outward, the child was hurting regardless of what Amy might do next.

Amy grimaced. "How long ago did this happen?"

His mother, Shawna, answered. "'Bout a week. More or less." Thanks to hard living and a husband who drank, she appeared much older than her early thirties. In spite of the obvious lack of funds, her children were clean, though their clothes were threadbare. The kitchen was separated from the so-called living room by the placement of two aged recliners and a sofa rather than a wall, so it was easy to see how she kept her drab little house spotless.

"What did you cut yourself with?" she asked Tony.

"A lid from a tin can," was his tremulous reply.

His mother interrupted. "If I told them kids once, I told 'em a hundred times not to play near the trash. But do they ever listen?" Shawna glared at her line-up of children, forcing them to hang their heads in shame.

So much for hoping Tony's injury had been caused by something clean. "Was it rusty?"

"Mighta been."

She glanced up at Shawna. "When was his last tetanus shot?"

"Couple years ago. Do ya think he's gettin' lockjaw?"

"No, but Tony needed stitches and an antibiotic. You should have brought him to me sooner," Amy said. Although it was too late for Tony, perhaps Shawna wouldn't make the same mistake if something like this happened to one of her other children.

"I couldn't. Anyways, I had him keep it clean so I figgered it would be all right. Made him wear his shoes, too."

Amy glanced at the rest of Tony's brothers and sisters who'd lined up in the kitchen to watch. The four were equally dark-haired and ranged in size and age like steps, starting with the oldest girl at twelve and the youngest boy at four. Each of them was barefoot and completely tanned from spending most of their summer outdoors.

"I'm afraid he's not all right," Amy said, trying to clean out the wound as best she could. "He's developed an infection that needs medical attention."

Shawna nodded. "That's why I called you. I knew you'd come and give him some pills or a salve or somethin'."

"He needs more than a few pills and ointment," Amy insisted. "We're talking intravenous antibiotics if we want to save his foot. With his diabetes, you can't afford to ignore this injury and hope it will get better on its own."

Shawna wrung her hands in apparent indecision, at the same time glancing toward a closed door. "You really think he needs to go to the hospital?"

"Yes, I do," Amy said firmly. "The longer you keep Tony at home, the worse he'll get."

"I don't have a way to get him there—" Shawna began.

"My car's parked at the curb." Amy rewrapped Tony's foot with a clean bandage from her bag. Satisfied with her efforts, she stripped off her gloves and withdrew her ear thermometer to check for a fever. His skin was warm to the touch and his temperature was well above normal.

"If one of you will bring my bag, I'll carry Tony to my car." She helped the boy steady himself as he rose and stood like a flamingo. Before he could take his first hop, the closed door swung open with a bang and Yancy Mullen stumbled through, his sleeveless shirt unbuttoned.

"What's going on?" he yelled, hitching up his jeans as he scratched at his overhanging belly. "A man can't sleep around here with all the noise."

Shawna and her children froze. The fear on their faces

was unmistakable. "We tried to be quiet, Yancy. You can go on back to bed if'n you want."

"I'm awake now," he roared. Rubbing his bewhiskered face, he narrowed his red eyes to study Amy. "Who the hell are you?"

"I'm Amy Wyman," she said as the odor of alcohol wafted in her direction. "Your wife called me to look at your son. I'm a nurse," she tacked on, using a title which was probably more familiar to him.

He glanced at Tony. "What's wrong with you, boy?"

"N-nothing," he stammered.

Yancy waved at him. "Then git on outa here. Find something to do."

Although Tony made every attempt to obey, Amy gripped his arm and tethered him beside her. "Tony's foot is infected. He needs to be in the hospital."

Yancy glared at his wife. "Did you call another one of those do-gooders to come and interfere again?"

Shawna didn't meet his gaze. "Tony is sick."

"And you baby the boy too much. I'm already spending my hard-earned money on the medicine you claim he needs. Insulin, bah!" He spat on her spotless floor.

"Tony is a diabetic and needs the medication," Amy broke in. "Because of his condition, we have to take extra care of this infection."

"Then give him some pills or a shot or somethin'. The boy's used to shots by now."

"He needs a hospital. I'm taking him."

Built like a football player who'd gone to seed, Yancy still moved fast. "Like hell you are. You can't take my kid without my permission."

Size-wise, he could easily stop her. She might be small, but people usually responded to the calm authority in her voice. Although Yancy seemed beyond rational thought at the moment, she had to reason with him. "Your wife is coming along."

"Like hell she is!" Had Amy ever heard a bull roar, she would have assumed the noise resembled the man bellowing in front of her.

"Mr Mullen," she began. "Tony could die without treatment."

His beady eyes seemed to grow smaller. "Says you."

"All right," she said evenly. "Let's take him to the emergency room. A doctor will tell you the same thing."

"I ain't paying for no 'mergency room and no doctors. They're all a bunch of quacks anyways."

"They'll try to save your son's life. He needs more care than you can give at home."

Yancy turned back to his wife. "Didn't I tell you to soak his foot in Epsom salt water? If'n you had, he'd be fine."

Shawna wrung her hands. "I did, Yancy. It didn't do no good."

"Because Tony needs an antibiotic," Amy interrupted. "A salt-water soak isn't the answer. You don't want him to lose his foot, do you?"

"My parents used Epsom salts for everything and they got by without any highfalutin, high-paid doctors."

"Then they were lucky."

He folded his beefy arms over his belly. "What's good enough for them is good enough for me and mine."

Trying to reason with him wasn't getting her, or Tony, anywhere. She hoped that for all of Yancy's bluster, he wouldn't hurt her or his family.

"If you think I'm causing trouble now," Amy said in a voice for his ears only, "then wait until Social Services hear how you've refused medical treatment for your child."

A feral gleam filled his eyes and he slowly shook his head. "You ain't gonna tell nobody nothing."

"That's where you're wrong, Mr Mullen," Amy said.

"I'm going to sing like a canary if I leave here without Tony. And since you're endangering the health and life of a child, you'd better believe that the police will be knocking on your door before you can pop the top on another beer can."

"Yer bluffin'."

"No, I'm not."

"Well, I don't bluff neither, Miss Can't-Mind-Her-Own-Business." He glanced around the room. "Where's my gun?"

The time for a hasty exit had arrived, especially when he disappeared into the other room.

"You'd better go," Shawna whispered. "I hid it, but he'll find it. He always does."

"I'm not leaving without Tony. It isn't safe for you either."

"He won't hurt us. Just go." She pushed them forward while her other children stared at them with fear on their faces. The four-year-old began to cry and the oldest snatched him close to soothe him.

Although Tony weighed about eighty pounds, Amy half carried him to the front door. She'd nearly made it before she heard the distinctive sound of Yancy loading his shotgun.

"I done told you. You ain't goin' nowheres with my boy."

Instantly the children ran outside. The door banged in their hurry to escape, leaving her, Tony and Shawna to face his wrath. Amy hoped they would summon help and not wait for the situation to resolve itself. If only she could have signaled one of them to use her car phone.

The sight of the shotgun barrel pointed at her made her mouth go dry, but she refused to act cowed. Men like Yancy Mullen thrived on intimidating those whom they considered weaker than themselves. She crossed her fingers, hoping Shawna was right about Yancy not harming them. "Tony needs a doctor."

Yancy motioned her away from the door. "Have a seat. If the wife thought you could fix him up, then you'd better get busy."

"I did what I could. Tony needs more than what I brought in my bag."

"Well, now, I guess we have us a dilemma. You ain't leavin' with him, and since you said you ain't leaving *without* him, you might as well just make yourself comfortable. If he's as sick as you say he is, you'll be here for quite a spell."

Amy wanted to stamp her feet in frustration. "He won't *get* better without the proper antibiotics. Why don't you come with us and hear what the doctor says for yourself?"

"You people stick together," he accused.

"I'll call a friend of mine—"

He cut Amy off before she completed her sentence. "You ain't callin' nobody, so just sit yerself down and hush up."

Knowing she wouldn't make any progress by arguing, Amy guided Tony to the sofa and sat beside him. Someway, somehow she would get out of this mess and take Tony with her. If one of the Mullen children found a phone and called the police, she'd be all right, but in case they didn't, she had to devise a plan.

"I need another beer," Yancy announced from his place at the kitchen table where he could easily observe everyone's moves.

Shawna went to the refrigerator, removed a can and set it on the table before she returned to the sofa. Gathering her son against her, she waited.

He popped the top and guzzled the contents. A minute later, he smacked his lips. "Gonna be a long night," he commented before he took another swallow.

Amy glanced at her watch. It was nearly seven-thirty. Ryan wouldn't worry about her until almost nine. A lot could happen in the meantime if Yancy's beer supply ran out. If only she could call Ryan...

As soon as Yancy drained the can, he crushed it with one huge hand. "Do you need another one?" Shawna asked.

"Might as well. Can't do nuthin' else," he muttered.

Being helpful, Shawna pulled out two cans from the refrigerator and set them both in front of him. Before she could walk across the room, he'd guzzled his second and started on the third.

"He'll pass out soon," Shawna whispered. "Then you can go."

Before Amy could nod, Yancy yelled at her, "No talkin'. A body can't hear himself think."

The wail of a siren came close and Amy breathed a sigh. Her relief was short-lived, however, because the noise died some distance away, as if the cruiser had been summoned elsewhere.

Yancy staggered to his feet and stumbled toward the front window. Pushing the curtain aside, he looked out. "Wonder what's goin' on? Damn neighbors. Cops are always around for one thing or 'nuther."

Amy had hoped the law had come for *them*, but as Yancy returned to his seat, apparently appeased by what he hadn't seen, her optimism died.

A few minutes later, a voice seemed to surround the house. "Yancy Mullen. This is the police. Throw down your weapon and come out with your hands raised."

Amy looked heavenward and sent up a prayer of thanks, noticing how Shawna appeared to do the same.

Yancy bounded to his feet, cursing a blue streak. "What the hell—?" He went to the window and shouted, "Forget it. I ain't comin' out."

"Then let the people inside walk away," the voice on the loudspeaker said.

"Not a chance. Just stay clear of us. Do ya hear me?"

"Let everyone go. We'll talk," said the voice.

"Well, talk this." With that, he pulled the trigger and sent a blast of buckshot through the ceiling.

# CHAPTER EIGHT

SHAWNA screamed, Tony cried out and Amy flung herself over the boy while plaster rained down on them.

All Amy could think was that if she got through this unscathed, Ryan would kill her for making a house call.

Then again, it was entirely possible that she might not even see him again. Fear reared its head and she bit her lip. Stay calm, she told herself. Somehow she'd find a way to get them out of this mess, or at least keep everyone alive until the men outside were able to subdue Yancy.

As soon as the worst of the dust cleared, she raised herself to check on Tony and Shawna. "Are you OK?"

Tony sniffled and his mother nodded.

Nothing happened for several minutes. Amy took deep breaths to relax, then coughed as the dusty air filled her lungs.

Finally, Yancy spoke, sounding pleased with himself. "Showed them, didn't I?"

"You're gonna get us all killed, you fool," Shawna railed at him through her tears. "All we wanted to do was take Tony to the hospital. Now you're in a whole mess of trouble."

"I ain't having nobody tell me how to take care of my family," he shouted at her, holding his shotgun loosely with one hand. "Now hush up, so's I can think."

Amy reached across Tony to place her hand on Shawna's arm. "Don't antagonize him," she whispered. "Once he calms down, maybe we can reason with him." She hadn't been able to break through his alcohol-induced anger before, but that had been before the police had surrounded the house. With his options so plainly limited, surely he would listen to her now.

Shawna slowly nodded, her expression resigned. Tony's quiet sobs demanded her attention and she held him close, whispering in his ear.

An hour passed. Then another. Yancy refused all requests to allow the police access or for any of them to leave. Amy acted with Shawna and Tony as if she were a guest and they were simply enjoying each other's company. Shadows inside the house started to deepen as the sun's rays faded. Amy's hopes for a speedy resolution experienced the same fate.

"Turn on some lights," Yancy ordered. His wife complied by clicking on the lamp beside the sofa.

The tension in the room grew thicker and Amy doubted if the knots in her stomach would ever go away. She rubbed her neck and flexed her shoulders, wondering when the SWAT team would make their move.

Before she could dwell on the thought, both the front and back doors burst open. Armed SWAT team members swarmed in, garbed head to toe in their distinctive black gear, weapons drawn. With Yancy's reflexes dulled, he didn't have time to grab his shotgun off the table.

"Don't touch it," one officer ordered as the other two moved into position to protect her, Tony and Shawna.

As if aware he was outnumbered and outgunned, Yancy surrendered. Immediately, two policemen cuffed his hands behind his back while another read him his rights.

An officer who'd stationed himself in front of Amy asked, "Are any of you hurt?"

Amy found her voice and noticed it sounded as shaky as her knees. "Thank God you came when you did. We're fine. Tony needs to go to the hospital, though."

"An ambulance is outside," he told her.

The drama over, the officers led Yancy out of the house

to a waiting police car. Shawna's other children rushed in, wide-eyed, as if they weren't sure what they would find. Shawna opened her arms to hold them all close as she burst into tears.

Amy wanted to do the same now that the excitement was over, but someone had to talk to the police, make arrangements for Tony and take care of a hundred other little details. The time for falling apart would have to wait.

"We called the police, Mama," the middle daughter told her. "Daddy's gonna be mad at us, isn't he?"

"Yes, but it don't matter." Shawna wiped her face with her fingers. "Come on. Let's take your brother to the hospital."

"I'll carry him, ma'am," one of the officers told her. Hefting the boy in his arms as if he weighed no more than a small sack of sugar, he left the house with Tony's brothers and sisters following.

"What are you going to do?" Amy asked Shawna. "You don't have to live like this."

She shrugged, looking extremely tired. "I know. I kept hoping things would get better, but I don't expect they will. It's time I face facts and figure out something else for me and my kids."

"The local family crisis center will help," Amy told her. "The police will put you in contact with them if you ask."

The other woman nodded. "I will."

Amy walked out of the house with her arm around Shawna's thin shoulders, not sure who was supporting whom. From out of the darkness someone called her name and she stopped to glance around. To her surprise, Ryan appeared out of the shadows and slowly swung himself toward her on his crutches.

As he came closer to the circle of light created by the porch's bare bulb, she noticed his set jaw and the grim determination on his features. Seeing his concern and knowing what he must have gone through to be here, her façade of strength began to crumble and tears began flowing down her face.

Tears of relief.

He stopped and dropped one crutch to hold out an arm. Amy left Shawna and walked directly into his embrace. For the first time since she'd walked into the Mullens' house, she felt her stress ease and she melted against him. He held her with her head tucked under his chin until she stopped shaking and the fountain inside her dried to a trickle.

"I heard the gunshot," he said.

"We're OK," she said. "I was afraid I might never see you again."

"That makes two of us."

She pulled away slightly. "How did you know what was happening? And how did you get here?"

"Dora called. How I got here isn't important. The question is, have you lost all good sense?" His voice rose as if now that she was out of harm's way, he intended to scold her within an inch of her life.

"No, I—"

"You could have been killed. Why didn't you tell me what you were going to do?"

"I didn't expect this to happen on a routine house call," she said in her defense.

"You still should have told me."

"You don't need to yell," she retorted. "I've had enough of that tonight, thank you very much."

He drew a deep breath as if struggling for control. "I'm sorry but, my God, woman, do you realize what I went through...?" His voice faded.

Before she knew it, he kissed her.

This wasn't a kiss of passion, Amy realized, but one to reassure himself that she had made it through this evening in one piece. His lips were hard against hers and he clutched her as if he couldn't let go. Surrounded by his warmth, she couldn't think of any place she'd rather be than in the comfort and safety of his arms.

A few seconds later, he raised his head to stare intently at her. "Are you really OK?"

She nodded. "Yes."

His gaze didn't waver. "You're sure."

Physically, she was, but emotionally? She wasn't certain. "I should be asking you that question. You have no business being out here when you had surgery this morning. You should be resting."

"I had a long nap," he said. "Are you ready to go home?"

She sighed, rubbing the back of her neck as she pushed aside the image of the shotgun barrel pointed at her. "Not yet. I have to give my statement to the police. Tony has to be admitted and Shawna needs a place—"

"Give them your statement," he said. "I'll call in Jackson to take care of Tony."

"And Shawna and her family?"

"According to the police chief, Yancy will be in jail for some time. If the judge sets bail, the amount will be high enough that I doubt if Yancy can pay it. Shawna won't have to worry about him bothering her or the kids. They'll be able to stay here at home and get their lives in order."

She watched as Shawna's neighbors, a couple in their forties, approached to talk to her while the ambulance attendants strapped Tony onto a gurney. "Yes, but I want to make sure before I go home."

Amy left Ryan on the sidewalk to talk to Tony's mother. The neighbors had agreed to drive her to the hospital and keep an eye on the other children. After reassuring them that Tony would receive excellent attention from both the ER physician and Dr Jackson, she searched out Ryan. He was leaning against the hood of the nearest patrol car, talking to a policeman.

"Ms Wyman?" the officer asked. "Could you, please, tell us what happened?"

Aware of Ryan standing nearby, she drew a deep breath before outlining the events. When she mentioned the part about Yancy shooting a hole in the ceiling, she could feel the tension radiating from him. She finished with, "Then the cavalry arrived."

After another hour of waiting, completing paperwork and signing the necessary complaint forms, she was free to leave.

"You wouldn't tell me before, but how did you get here?" she asked Ryan on the way to her car.

"I pulled a few strings and came with the ambulance crew in case someone needed a doctor. Now I'm going to catch a ride with you. If you're not up to driving, the patrolman said he'd take us home."

"I'm fine," she said again, willing away the slight tremor in her hands.

They traveled to Ryan's house in silence, for which Amy was grateful. Talking seemed to take more energy than she possessed at the moment.

"Park at your place," he ordered. "I'll walk."

"Don't be ridiculous," she said. "I've driven across town so I can surely manage a turn around the block."

When she pulled into his driveway, the outside light, triggered by the vehicle's motion, clicked on and the shadows inside her car disappeared.

"You look a little pale. Are you sure you're OK?" he asked.

She forced a smile, feeling as if she were a rubber band about to snap. "You've already asked me several times. I'm fine." Or she would be once she got home.

"If you need to talk, you know where to find me."

Nodding, she asked, "Shall I walk you to your door?"

"I can find my way," he said, hauling himself and his crutches out of the vehicle. "Good night."

"Good night," she echoed, eager to go home.

Although Amy was surrounded by the familiar, her tremors didn't disappear. Concentrating on routine tasks helped, but even after she'd crawled into bed she couldn't sleep. The image of Yancy pointing his shotgun, the sharp sound of the weapon firing, the acrid smell of the blast and the taste of fear in her mouth replayed themselves no matter what she focused on to occupy her thoughts.

Giving up, she padded to the living-room sofa in her bare feet. Although it was well past two a.m., she telephoned the hospital to check on Tony.

"You're the second person to ask," the night nurse revealed. "Dr Gregory hung up a few minutes ago."

So he was still awake, too. A warm glow spread through her as she contemplated his thoughtfulness. Or was he merely checking on his colleague?

"Tony's mother is sleeping in his room," the nurse continued. "Would you like to talk to her?"

"Don't wake her," Amy said, conscious of how mentally and physically drained Shawna must be. "Just tell her I called. I'll drop by tomorrow."

After she hung up, she curled up on one corner of her overstuffed sofa, clutched the giant teddy bear she'd won at a carnival and tucked her toes under Mindy's warm body.

All she needed now was to suck her thumb, she thought as she began to shake like a leaf ready to fall off a tree.

As nights went, it hadn't been one of her better evenings, but it was certainly one she would never forget.

"Should I call Ryan?" she asked Mindy, suddenly craving the sound of his voice.

The spaniel immediately sat up and turned her head toward the kitchen.

"I take it that's a yes," she commented.

Mindy bounded off the sofa and ran into the other room, her toenails clicking on the linoleum.

Amy picked up the phone which rested on the end table beside her. "I'm phoning." She raised her voice to tell her pet. "We're not visiting."

Mindy replied with a woof and the whimper she used when she wanted to go outside. Before Amy could recall her dog, she heard a brisk knock on her sliding glass patio door.

She tentatively trailed after Mindy and cautiously opened the vertical blinds to reveal Ryan standing on the other side, wearing a pair of athletic shorts and a souvenir St Louis T-shirt. Although he was using his crutches, he also carried a silver flask by a leather strap. Another bark reminded her to let him in.

"I saw your light was on," he said without preamble as he swung himself over the threshold. "Can't sleep?"

"No," she admitted, happy to see him. Having another person in the same house made her feel infinitely better. Not just any person, she corrected herself. *Ryan.*

"I didn't think you would. Which is why I brought a little something to help you deal with the shock." He raised the flask.

"Considering how alcohol contributed to my nightmare, I don't want to drown my problems."

"Who said anything about drowning?" he asked, moving toward the cabinets near the sink. "You're only getting a shot of brandy for medicinal purposes. Where are your glasses?"

"The door on your right," she told him.

He removed a small juice glass and splashed in about an ounce. Handing it to her, he said, "Bottom's up."

She eyed the liquid, then tossed it down in one smooth

gulp. Ryan smiled as she coughed and sputtered. "Feeling better?"

"Not really," she croaked.

"You will," he reassured her. He, on the other hand, probably wouldn't. After seeing her cotton top hug her curves and what seemed like miles of smooth, tanned and heart-stoppingly bare skin, he wished his pain pill would lessen the ache occurring in parts farther north of his ankle.

He'd manage, though, because Amy needed him.

"Now, it's off to bed for you," he said firmly.

"You're not leaving already, are you?"

The frantic note in her voice made him smile. "I'll stay until you fall asleep. How's that?"

He read the relief in her slumped shoulders and thankful expression. "The bedroom's down the hall. Are you sure you don't want a shot of brandy yourself? Or some tea?"

She was obviously afraid to close her eyes and was doing everything she could to stall. "I'll be right next to you," he promised.

Ryan followed her through the living room and caught a glimpse of a giant teddy bear tossed haphazardly on the sofa. Her furnishings were a combination of new and old, as if she purchased pieces to suit her mood rather than to fit into a particular decorating style. An antique pie safe with elaborate carvings stood in one corner while a plain bookcase took up space in another.

He carefully maneuvered himself through the narrow hallway, trying to watch his step as the sway of her hips attracted his attention like a child's to candy. It didn't get easier once he entered the bedroom.

Lacy white curtains, a lilac-print comforter thrown back to reveal pale purple sheets and an array of blue and purple pillows strewn across the floor made it plain that this particular room's occupant was a woman. A matching lilac tablecloth covered a small round table in one corner.

Several fat candles and a basket of flowers rested on top, scenting the air with the fragrance he associated with Amy.

"I'll give you the left side," she said, tugging the comforter off the full-sized bed.

He'd planned on *sitting* beside her, not *lying* beside her on a mattress that was adequate for a single person and extremely cozy for two. Without a chair in sight and hardly any space to accommodate one, he had no choice. He couldn't deny her request, neither did he want to. Swallowing hard, he propped his crutches against the wall and longed for the swig of brandy he'd refused earlier.

As he lowered himself to sit on the bed with the pillow propped behind his back, he couldn't stop a sigh from escaping his mouth. His mind might not be able to shut down, but his body was more than ready to relax. At least it was until Amy switched off the bedside lamp and slid under the top sheet.

"This is crazy," she said, "but I can't seem to stop shaking."

Knowing that she needed his touch for reassurance as much as he did, he gave in and stretched out next to her. He extended his right arm in a silent offer to hold her. Without hesitation, she wiggled against him as if it were the most natural thing to do. Her silky hair flowed across his arm as she rested her head on his shoulder. It seemed a perfect fit.

He didn't say a word. If she needed to talk, he would listen, but the choice was hers. Certainly, she needed to relax, so he let his fingers speak for him. He caressed her from the top of her head to as far as he could reach, feeling the stiffness in her jaw and tremors shaking her entire body. She felt unusually cold in spite of the warm evening and he continued his soothing touch until she stopped trembling.

Mindy took that moment to trot in and lay on the throw

rug near the bed. Ryan hoped he wouldn't trip over her when he slipped out later.

Amy placed her hand on his chest and he stiffened. "How did you know I couldn't sleep?" she asked.

He drew a deep breath and willed the blood racing around his body to slow down. Concentrate on talking and not feeling, he told himself.

"I couldn't either," he admitted honestly, remembering the sound of the shotgun blast. He'd never felt so helpless before in his life. "I even called the hospital to check on Tony. He's resting comfortably."

"I must have called shortly after you did because the nurse told me the same thing," she revealed. "Were you satisfied with Josh's treatment plan?"

"I didn't ask about that."

He heard a distinct pause. "You didn't?" she asked.

"No."

"Why not?"

He hesitated. "I wondered why myself. As I thought about it, I realized how strongly you must have felt about Tony's condition to fight against his father, who was armed and dangerous. But when it was all over, you didn't balk at placing Tony in Josh's hands. If you could do that, I couldn't do any less."

"So you trust him."

He felt her nod of satisfaction. "I'm trying," he said.

"I'm glad," she said simply. "But if you didn't call to check out his care…?"

"I called because Tony had been through a lot. If he was agitated or upset, then I wanted to know so we could bring in a counselor or the chaplain to talk to the family."

"I hadn't thought of that," she said slowly. "I'd been more concerned about the physical and had overlooked his emotional needs. How sweet of you."

He smiled at her praise. "Just doing my job. Anyway,

he's fine, but they'll arrange for a counselor to see him in the morning.''

Once again, he felt her nodding. "You never explained why *you* couldn't sleep," she said. "Was your foot bothering you?"

He shook his head. "The only thing disturbing me was the very real possibility that Yancy could have missed the ceiling and hit you.''

She sat up to stare at him and spoke in a teasing tone. "Why, Dr Gregory. I'm surprised you cared.''

"Sure. Good NPs are hard to find.'' He sounded gruff even to himself. Yet, even as he spoke, some part of him knew he hadn't totally told the truth. Yes, he'd been concerned for her just as he would have been for any staff member, but the fear he'd experienced over Yancy harming Amy had gone much deeper, as if he might have lost more than a colleague. Was this the love his grandfather and father talked about, or was it purely physical attraction? He'd have to think about it when she wasn't draped over him like a blanket and he was more in control.

"Anyway, don't let it go to your head," he said lightly.

His eyes had adjusted to the darkness, but the moon's glow and a streetlamp allowed him to see her smile. "I won't." She snuggled against him once again.

"How did a nice girl like you end up being a clown?" he asked.

"I just fell into it," she answered. "I met Sunny and she mentioned how she was looking for someone to occasionally fill in for her hospital visits. It sounded like fun, so I agreed. Learning the tricks was the hardest part because Sunny was so adept.''

He thought of the hours he'd spent practicing the coin trick he'd shown her. "I know.''

"Who taught you how to pull a coin out of thin air?"

"My mom. She liked being the life of the party." Unwilling to discuss his family, he changed the subject. "So tell me about the Mullens."

She stiffened slightly, then relaxed. "We diagnosed Tony with diabetes shortly after I came to Maple Corners. His father didn't believe he was ill and he certainly wasn't willing to pay for the insulin. I worked with a social worker and was able to arrange for the state to issue Tony a medical card."

"So what's Yancy's problem? He didn't have to spend any of his own money on his son's care."

"No, but Yancy doesn't like having outsiders interfere in what he calls 'family business'. He hated it when Shawna brought the kids to us for treatment so, instead of begging him to bring them, she'd usually ask if I'd make a house call when he wasn't home."

"But he was."

"This time, yes," she said wryly. "If I'd gone tomorrow morning, I probably would have missed him. After I heard Shawna describe what Tony's foot looked like, I thought my visit was worth the risk. I was afraid of what I'd find if I waited another twelve hours."

"You should have taken one of us or—"

"Like who? You weren't in any shape to go anywhere. Dora couldn't go—I'd asked her. I couldn't find Josh. I had no idea Yancy would wake up from his nap."

"Don't walk into something like that again."

"Hmm," she answered.

Ryan squeezed her. "I'm serious, Amy."

"I know you are, but I can't ignore someone's request for help because I'm afraid. The odds are probably one in a million of this ever happening again."

"They had better be," he muttered. Then, playing on a hunch, he asked, "Do you make other house calls?"

She paused, clearly debating if she should tell the truth

or not. "On occasion. The home situations are completely different to the Mullens'."

"I should hope so. You scared about ten years off my life tonight."

She giggled. "Mine, too."

For several minutes, he only heard the usual sounds of the house creaking and a faint snuffle as Mindy dreamed her doggy dreams. His own eyelids felt heavy and he relaxed.

Before long, Amy yawned. "I think the brandy is working."

"That's good." He tried to summon the energy to rise, but couldn't. A few more minutes, he thought. She'd be asleep and he could go home to his cold and lonely bed.

"Tell me about your parents," she said.

"There's not much to tell. They're divorced and are much happier apart than they were together."

"So it wasn't an amicable parting of the ways?"

"Hardly. I was shuffled back and forth so they each had equal time, and I hated it. Neither of them trusted the other and I learned early that it wasn't the kind of life I wanted. If they hadn't been set up with each other as a blind date, their paths would never have crossed. I'm amazed they were able to carry on a conversation much less consider getting married. They were total opposites."

His father had warned him during one of their man-to-man talks to find a woman with his head and not his hormones. Lust and love weren't the same thing, he'd cautioned. Because his father had apparently not discovered that difference until it had been too late, Ryan had vowed not to make the same mistake.

However, that had been before Amy had walked into his life. Right now, having her plastered against him, it seemed as if they wouldn't encounter any problem too insurmountable. The little voice in his head reminded him of how the disparity in their personalities was a recipe for disaster but he quieted the thought with a stern warning.

"Maybe they thought they could change each other. Or maybe they couldn't find enough common ground to build a relationship."

"Probably." His mother had railed at his father for not sharing her interests, while his dad had responded in kind. They'd spent less and less time together until finally his mother had filed for a divorce.

"That's too bad. I saw the picture of Arlington Cemetery in your office. Does the site have a special significance to you?"

"My grandfather's buried there. He had me for a whole summer once and we had a great time. Gramps knew what life with my parents was like and he tried to help me put things in perspective. I do miss him."

His grandfather had been the one who'd listened to his troubles and had responded by telling him happy stories of his life with Ryan's grandmother in "the good old days". Ryan had taken his advice to "marry someone whose faults you can live with" to heart. Between Gramps's and his dad's well-meant counsel, he'd remained single while patting himself on the back for avoiding the cycle of marriage and divorce that his friends had already experienced.

Lying in bed with Amy, though, it made him realize what his caution had cost him. He turned onto his side and settled against her, spoon fashion. The darkness made it far too easy to pretend that he and the woman in his arms were meant to be together. For the first time in his life he truly understood how his father must have felt when he, as a quiet man, had attracted the attention of a beautiful, vivacious young lady.

"I'm glad you had someone to talk to," she murmured.

Surrounded by her warmth and filled with a contented

lethargy, Ryan's last conscious hope was for morning to be a long time coming.

The distinctive warble of the cardinal who lived in the evergreen outside Amy's bedroom window woke her. Before she opened her eyes, she knew it was morning. Hating the idea of leaving her cozy nest, she let herself enjoy the cocoon of warmth around her. She'd slept much better than she'd expected, and she owed it all to Ryan.

Thinking of Ryan, she instantly became aware of his form still resting beside her, one arm flung around her middle, his breath against the back of her neck. They'd talked for hours and he'd obviously lulled himself to sleep in spite of his intentions to stay only until she'd dozed off.

Underneath his businesslike demeanor, he really was a sweet, caring man. Their conversations last night, both before and after her house-call fiasco, had helped her understand why he held himself aloof from others.

His life experiences had taught him the pain of trusting another person, both personally and professionally. Scaling his inherent wall of mistrust was daunting to say the least, but she had climbed a few of those bricks. His willingness to trust Dr Jackson was a victory of sorts and she was determined to keep pushing until she'd reduced that wall to rubble.

The phone jarred her totally awake. Twisting herself out from under Ryan's arm to reach for it, she noticed two things. The sun was extraordinarily bright and the digital clock display read nine a.m. Cursing under her breath, she answered.

''Are you coming to work this morning?'' Tess asked.

''I overslept,'' she said, rubbing her eyes. ''I'll be there in a few minutes.''

''Do you know if Dr Gregory will be in at all today?''

Tess asked. "I have a lady who insists on seeing a doctor as soon as possible."

Amy eyed the man beside her who'd raised himself on one elbow as he studied her. He looked incredibly sexy with his hair mussed and a shadow of whiskers on his face. "I'm not sure what he's going to do."

As if aware he was being discussed, Ryan leaned closer to whisper in her ear. "I'll be in this afternoon. If someone can't wait, send him over to Josh."

Tess's voice filled her other ear. "Maybe I should just call him myself."

"No, don't." Knowing Tess wouldn't reach him, she didn't want her guessing where he might be. Amy quickly revised his message. "Refer the lady to Dr Jackson. If Dr Gregory comes in, he probably won't make it until this afternoon."

She quickly replaced the receiver before Tess could ask more questions.

"Why didn't you tell her what I'd said?" he asked.

"Because she'd wonder how I knew your plans when thirty seconds ago I had no idea. It will save us both a lot of questions if we don't broadcast where you spent last night."

"Good idea," he admitted. "How did you sleep?"

Warmth spread across her face. "Wonderfully. And you?"

"The best since before my accident. I'm sorry I didn't leave, but once I relaxed I guess everything caught up with me."

"I didn't mind." Amy smiled. "It was nice having my own personal heating pad."

She wondered if the faint pink on his face was due to embarrassment or a trick of the sunlight. "I didn't crush you with my leg, did I?" he asked, changing the subject.

"Not at all." Apparently Ryan had trouble with

mornings-after. His disquiet was quaint and old-fashioned, considering how this technically wasn't a *morning-after* in the usual sense of the word.

She wished that it had been.

He swung his feet over the edge of the mattress and reached for his crutches. "I'd better go."

Before he could lever himself off the bed, she hurried around to stand in front of him. Without giving herself time to contemplate her actions, she pressed her mouth to his and hugged him.

"What was that for?" he asked, his face registering both surprise and pleasure.

"Several things," she said lightly. "First, to thank you for being here when I needed you."

"It worked both ways," he told her soberly.

"And my second reason was because…" She drew a deep breath before plunging in. "I wanted to."

# CHAPTER NINE

A SLOW grin spread across Ryan's face. "I'm glad you did. I wanted the same thing."

The doubt Amy had felt over her impulsive gesture quickly faded. She'd always believed in going after what was in her heart, and her sisters had encouraged her to do so. "What are you doing this weekend?" she asked as an idea formed.

"Gee, I don't know." He glanced at his leg with a wry expression. "Surely there's a ten-kilometer race I could enter."

"Seriously," she lightly scolded.

"I'm sure I'll find something to stumble around the house and do."

"How does an outdoor concert sound? The city band is scheduled to perform tonight."

"Sounds good."

"Then it's settled," she said, delighted to share another evening with him. "I'll see you at six-thirty."

He rose and placed the crutches under his arms. "Oh, you'll see me before then. I'll be at work as soon as I can get ready."

"Why?" she asked. "We've rescheduled your patients and Dr Jackson agreed to cover for you."

"Consider this a trial run for next week," he said, making his way down the hall and into her kitchen.

"All right, but take your time."

He stopped at the patio door. "I will." Leaning on his crutches, he peered at her. "Maybe you should be the one taking the day off."

She stared at him, incredulous. "Whatever for?"

"You've heard of post-traumatic stress?"

She waved her hand as if his suggestion were no more than a pesky fly. "I had that last night and now I'm fine. Thanks to you."

"OK, but if—"

"I know your phone number. And where you live," she added.

Apparently satisfied by her answer, he nodded, then stepped outside into the sunshine. Mindy followed and Amy watched the dog scramble down the steps while Ryan set a more sedate, deliberate pace. She hated to see him go, but at least she could look forward to seeing him the rest of the day.

After a quick shower, Amy hurried into the clinic shortly after nine-thirty with a huge smile on her face. "Looks like sleeping in added an extra bounce to your step," Tess commented.

"Oh, it did." Going into detail seemed tasteless, not to mention no one's business but her own.

"I heard about last night. It must have been horrible for you."

"It was," Amy agreed. "But all's well that ends well."

"How's the little boy?"

"I haven't checked with Dr Jackson yet this morning, but I'm going to right away."

"When you're finished, you have a couple of people waiting." Tess tapped the ledge where she placed the pending patient records.

"OK. I'll only be a minute." Amy went to her desk and telephoned Josh. "How's Tony doing?"

"I'm waiting for the culture report," he said. "The gram stain shows mixed flora, so I've put him on a broad-spectrum antibiotic. The lab will call me with a prelim this afternoon after they read the plates. If they find anything unusual, I'll adjust his medication accordingly.''

"He was feverish yesterday," she recalled.

"I ordered three sets of blood cultures," Josh reported. "According to the lab, their instrument can detect positives within six hours and so far the bottles have all shown no bacterial growth. If Tony hadn't come in when he did, though…" He didn't finish his comment and Amy imagined him shaking his head.

The thought of Tony fighting septicemia, along with his diabetes sent a shiver down her spine. Modern antibiotics worked wonders, but a lot of variables came into play. The fear of those few hours paled in comparison to the possibility of him losing his life.

"We're keeping a close eye on his blood sugars, too," Josh told her. "I've upped his insulin, so we'll see how he does."

"Thanks. Do you mind if I check in on him from time to time?"

She heard his shrug in his voice. "He was your patient. Feel free."

As she hung up, she suddenly realized how Ryan felt about turning his patients over to someone else's care. Maybe she shouldn't have judged him so harshly if she found herself monitoring their prescribed treatment, too.

The morning passed by quickly as she handled the usual cases of runny noses, sore throats, aches and pains. Her next patient was a mousy-haired woman in her forties who'd brought her recent lab work for review. Arlyss Drexal was about fifty pounds overweight and held down a sedentary job at a computer firm.

"I went to the health fair sponsored by the bank last week," Arlyss reported as she handed Amy several pages emblazoned with the Maple Corners Hospital logo. "There are a lot of numbers with an H beside them."

Amy scanned the records. Not only were Arlyss's cholesterol and triglyceride levels well above normal values, but her lipid profile also indicated an above-average risk for cardiac problems.

"Does this mean I'm going to have a heart attack?"

"If you continue your present lifestyle, yes, you run a greater chance of having a heart attack than the average person. Does anyone in your family have heart disease?"

Arlyss frowned. "No, but according to this, my history doesn't matter."

"Medicine isn't always an exact science. In your case, if you change your habits, you'll lower the possibility of having an MI. Remember, these tests are used as a screening tool to prevent disease."

"I suppose I could lose a few pounds," Arlyss mused.

Amy pointed to the body-mass index chart on the door. "Have you found your ideal weight range?"

Arlyss blanched at the figure posted. "That can't be right."

"These figures are a guide," Amy told her. "They'll give you something to aim for."

"How will I ever lose that much?" she wailed.

"Start walking. Take the stairs instead of the elevator. Join the health club. Attend aerobics classes. Bicycle. Find something to keep you moving. And no more donuts with your morning coffee."

Arlyss's mouth turned down. "I was afraid you'd say that. Eating celery and carrot sticks for breakfast, lunch and dinner isn't a happy picture."

Amy smiled. "There are several organized weight-loss programs available. I suggest you check them out and join one. Being in a group with others who are in the same boat, so to speak, will make it easier to stick to your diet."

"Diet." Arlyss made a face. "Just the word makes me cringe."

"Yes, but just imagine how wonderful you'll look by the time Christmas rolls around. You might be able to ask Santa for a new wardrobe."

Arlyss immediately brightened. "Do you think so?"

"Sure. You have six months. Piece of cake."

The older woman groaned. "Please. Don't mention cake."

"I won't," Amy promised. After she'd listened to her patient's heart and lungs and had pronounced her fit enough to begin an exercise regimen, she sent Arlyss on her way.

Entering the hallway, she ran into Ryan. "You made it," she teased.

Hanging on to his crutches, he shot her an exasperated glance. "Barely. Do you know how long it took me to take a shower and get dressed? I'll have to get up two hours earlier every morning so I won't be late."

"I'm sure you'll get faster as time goes on," she soothed.

"The next six weeks won't go by fast enough for me. I'll be in my office if you need me."

"Oh, by the way, the woman who called earlier asked to come in at two," Amy said.

"Do you know why she wanted an appointment?"

She shook her head. "Not a clue. I guess you can be surprised."

At two-ten, while she was in the process of returning phone calls, he approached her in her office. "Who's a good GI man?"

Amy leaned back in her chair. "Two gastroenterologists hold clinics at the hospital once or twice a month. Hoskins and Paige. I couldn't say if one is better than the other, though. Why?"

"Do you remember the patient who called this morning?" At her nod, he went on, "She wants a colonoscopy.

Apparently there's a history of colon cancer in her family and she wants a baseline.''

"Does Dora have any opinions?''

"Not really. According to her, Hoskins is more personable but either one is good.''

"I'll have to take her word for it because I haven't had any dealings with either of them,'' Amy admitted.

"OK. Whoever can give us the earliest appointment wins.''

Amy couldn't help but smile and pat herself on the back. She was making progress if he was willing to ask her opinion about a specialist.

The rest of the day passed by uneventfully, but Amy could hardly wait for the evening. Dora had left shortly after Ryan because she was going out of town to watch her son's baseball game. As Amy's last scheduled patient disappeared down the hallway, she grabbed her purse out of her bottom desk drawer.

"What's the rush?'' Tess asked, her eyebrows raised.

"Oh, Mom,'' Mollie moaned. "Can't you tell? She has a hot date.''

Amy stopped in her tracks. Mollie was either far too observant for a sixteen-year-old or she herself was acting much too eager. "I'm going out, yes.''

"Who's the studly guy?'' Mollie wanted to know.

Amy paused. "Who said anything about a stud?''

Mollie lifted one shoulder in a shrug. "I can't imagine you going out with anyone who wasn't.''

Amy was glad that Ryan wasn't within hearing distance. After he got over his initial embarrassment, Mollie's comment would probably go to his head. "I'm taking Dr Gregory to the concert. To get him out of the house,'' she added lamely.

Mollie shook her head. "Geez. Why would you waste

an evening with a hunk like him by hearing the local yokels play geek music?''

Tess shushed her daughter. ''Classical music is beautiful. Did you know that if babies listen to Mozart, their IQs improve? If I remember right, there's been research on how his compositions stimulate the learning centers in the brain.''

Mollie popped her gum. ''Like I said, *geek* music.''

''Actually,'' Amy said in a placating tone, ''we're going to hear jazz.''

''Take an umbrella,'' Tess advised. ''The forecast is for rain.''

''Only a twenty per cent chance,'' Mollie supplied. ''Which means there won't be a cloud in the sky.''

''Thanks for the advice,'' Amy said, edging her way to the door. ''Now, I'd better run so I have time to get ready.''

Tess grinned and Mollie winked, but Amy didn't stick around to answer any more questions.

By six-thirty, she had more clothes strewn across her bed than in the closet. She finally decided on her favorite pair of khaki shorts, a matching plaid short-sleeved shirt and sandals.

As the clock ticked on past the arranged time, she realized that she'd assumed Ryan would come to her house. It had been foolish on her part, considering how it would be much easier if she drove. Before she could call and tell him that she was on her way, her doorbell rang.

Ryan stood on the front step, looking quite handsome in his casual tan trousers and a navy blue polo shirt. ''Hi,'' he said. ''I forgot to ask if we'd need lawn chairs.''

''I have two ready and waiting.'' She motioned to the two webbed folding chairs propped against the wall. ''There are benches there, but I prefer sitting in the shade.''

''I'd offer to carry them, but I can barely handle these things,'' he said, motioning to his crutches.

"Not a problem," she said cheerfully.

Amy loaded the chairs in the back seat of his car, along with Ryan's crutches, and bit back her offer to act as chauffeur. The determination on his face as he slid behind the wheel told her he wouldn't have appreciated her suggestion.

A fair number of people had already gathered in front of the park's band shell by the time they arrived. Although the sun still shone, a line of dark clouds began to build to the west and the wind seemed stronger than before.

Amy scanned the park and chose what she thought was the perfect spot. It was shady and somewhat secluded, giving Ryan the space to stretch out his leg and not have anyone trip over his ankle by accident.

"Looks like we might get rain," he commented.

"Twenty per cent chance," she said, repeating Mollie's words. "It'll pass us by." Normally, she brought a blanket to sit on, but Ryan's injury made it impossible.

Although she'd purposely chosen an out-of-the-way location, the number of people who sauntered by to chat amazed her. Patients, neighbors and mere acquaintances meandered in their direction. By the time the band began tuning their instruments, she'd lost count.

Ryan leaned closer. "Phillip was right."

"About what?"

"He said you knew everyone in town. I'm inclined to believe him."

"Don't be silly."

"How *do* you know all these folks?"

"I like meeting people and so I do my best to get involved," she said.

"Did you ever think of a career in public relations?"

"Yes, but I thought I could do more good in medicine." The conductor took his place and waved his baton. "Oh, good. They're going to start."

The group wasn't bad considering it was composed of

nonprofessional musicians. However, by the time they'd played three selections, the sky had grown ominously dark, the wind now whipped the tops of the trees into a frenzy and an occasional flash of lightning split the sky.

A clap of thunder preceded the first fat droplets of rain. Within minutes, it turned into a downpour. People scattered to reach the safety of their vehicles.

Ryan dug in his pocket and handed over his keys before he rose. "Go on. I'll meet you at the car."

She folded the chairs. "I'm not leaving you, so don't waste time and energy arguing."

He moved as fast as he could, but even so she saw their shirts were soaking wet before she could unlock the doors.

"Get in," she ordered, pulling open the driver's door and taking his crutches. "Try to keep your cast dry."

"I think it's too late."

She ran to the other side, tossed her cargo into the back, then slid into the front passenger seat. "So much for our cultural event for the week."

"There'll be others. We should dry out before we do anything else this evening, don't you think?"

Her teeth chattered. "You're the doctor."

Ryan turned on the demister before he drove toward their housing development. The rain beat down so hard the wipers couldn't keep the windshield clear. He made an instant decision to take Amy to his place. Bypassing her street for his, he pulled into the driveway and activated his garage door.

"Aren't you taking me home?" she asked.

The heavy door slowly rose. "It's not a fit night to be out. You can wait at my place until it stops raining."

"I'm already wet."

He didn't need any reminders. Her shirt was plastered to her chest and the outline of her bra was clearly visible.

"You want to risk slipping on the concrete and breaking a bone? Or, worse, getting struck by lightning?"

A particularly brilliant flash illuminated the sky for a few seconds. "OK, OK. You've convinced me," she said.

"Smart lady."

"I don't have any clothes..."

He pushed aside the mental vision of Amy wearing only a towel. "I'll find something you can wear."

"OK." She rubbed her arms as he drove into the garage. Before he'd maneuvered himself from behind the wheel, she was waiting near the open door with his crutches.

"It's really a mess outside," she said as she stared at the rain dancing on the driveway and the water running like a river along the curb.

He stopped to glance into the darkness. The air already smelled cleaner. "How does Mindy handle storms?"

"She crawls under my bed at the first clap of thunder. She'll be fine."

He pressed the button to lower the door. "Come on. Let's get you dry."

Inside the house, he sat down to remove his shoe, then slogged toward his bedroom in a wet sock. "I'll find you something to wear," he called over his shoulder.

After rummaging through his closet, he found a velour bathrobe that he hadn't worn for ages. He tossed it over one shoulder before he turned and found her standing behind him.

She looked half-drowned. Her clothes clung to every curve and had become nearly invisible as wet fabric sometimes did. Her hair hung in long, dripping strands and the drops of moisture clinging to her skin glistened like pearls.

She was beautiful.

He swallowed hard and reluctantly handed her the robe. "Towels are in the bathroom. Take a hot shower or a bath."

She shook her head. "I want to check your cast first. Is it wet?"

"Probably."

Amy stepped forward. "Come on, buster. Drop 'em."

He'd never imagined taking his trousers off under these circumstances. "I can manage by myself."

"Fine. Do you have a hair-dryer?"

"No." He paused. "Wait. Check the bathroom. Mom may have left hers when she helped me move."

"I'll be back in a few minutes." She turned on one bare heel and Ryan instantly unzipped his trousers. If he'd read her stubborn expression correctly, she'd do the honors if he didn't. He wasn't willing to let her see his need for a cold shower.

He slipped on a pair of tracksuit pants because the zipper in the lower leg accommodated his cast. A whirring sound coming down the hallway told him she'd found a hair-dryer. He stripped off his shirt and drafted a clean T-shirt to serve as a towel.

Several minutes later, she re-entered, wearing his robe with the sleeves rolled up several times. Her hair now appeared only slightly damp rather than completely wet.

She brandished the hand-held dryer and passed a thick bath towel to him before she knelt at his feet. "Let's have a look."

While she inspected his cast, he dried his hair, then finger-combed the damp strands into place. "What's the verdict?"

"It's not as bad as I'd thought," she admitted. "Good thing you wore trousers instead of shorts."

"Yeah."

"A few minutes with this and you'll be good as new." She scrambled to find the electrical outlet and before long she was directing the warm air all over his cast.

Looking down, his mouth went dry. The neckline of his

robe gaped open, revealing one shoulder, miles of creamy skin and breasts that would fill his hands perfectly.

She shifted position and the robe parted at the hem. One knee poked through the opening before the long expanse of her thigh was revealed.

A combination of moan and anticipation had bubbled out of his throat before he'd realized it. She raised her head to stare at him. "Is this too hot?" she asked.

He swallowed hard. The heat he was experiencing had nothing to do with the hair-dryer's output. "No," he croaked. "Just…finish."

She returned to her task, oblivious to his turmoil. A sheen of sweat burst across his forehead and he wiped away the droplets before she could notice.

She tugged the robe back on her shoulder, but it slid off the other one, giving him a different perspective of the same view. He tried to study his family photo on the dresser, count the pennies lying next to his wallet, guess how much cologne was left in the bottle, but none of those things occupied his thoughts for long.

Ryan set his foot down. "That's enough," he said, rising to stand on his good foot.

She remained kneeling as she stared up at him. "What's wrong?"

"Nothing," he growled, unable to tear his attention away from her. "Everything."

Amy's gaze followed his and she glanced down at herself. Pink tinged her skin as she jumped up and retied the knot at her waist. "I wasn't trying to…to…"

He knew what she meant. "I know."

"It's not that I don't find you attractive. I do."

Her confession added fuel to his internal fire. Ryan reached out to stroke a strand of hair away from her face. When it came to medicine, he could talk circles around most people. Talking about his feelings was an entirely different story. He met her glance and let his appreciation of her beauty show.

She colored a darker shade of pink but made no effort to move away. Instead, he was certain he saw yearning in her eyes—the same yearning he felt deep inside.

He bent his head slowly, raising his eyebrows questioningly. This was her final opportunity to step back. She answered by closing her eyes and lifting her chin.

He touched his lips to hers, kissing her with as much tenderness as his banked passion would allow. He reached for the tie of her—his—robe and worked the bulky fabric free of its knot. His hands parted the fabric and moved to stroke every inch of her bared skin while his mouth trailed across her cheekbone.

"Are you sure you want this?" he murmured against her ear.

"Oh, yes," she breathed.

The rain beat against the windows and the roof as the storm unleashed its fury. From where Ryan stood, his desire for the woman in his arms threatened to explode at the same level of passion.

Eager to pull her onto the bed, without thinking he turned his body and shifted his weight to his weak leg. Unable to hold himself upright, he landed on the mattress with her tucked underneath him.

He muttered an expletive at his clumsiness—and at the sharp pain now shooting through his knee.

Thinking he'd injured himself, Amy froze. "Did you hurt something?" she asked, considering not only his ankle but also his knee and his back.

"I'm not sure."

Concern brought her out of her sensual lethargy. "Let me see," she said. "Don't move."

"Believe me, I won't."

She carefully untangled herself, taking the utmost care

not to jar him unnecessarily. "This is becoming a habit, you know."

"Don't remind me."

As soon as she was free, she knotted her robe closed and began running her hands down his left leg.

"What hurts?" she asked.

"Other than the obvious," he retorted, "my knee."

"Can you move it at all?"

He slowly straightened his leg, then rolled onto his back. "I'm OK. I just twisted the muscles."

She massaged the area. "How about an ice pack?"

"No. The pain's better already." He studied her. "Shall we continue where we left off?"

She wasn't totally convinced he hadn't injured himself and simply didn't want to admit it. "Maybe we should wait."

He paused, then pinched the bridge of his nose. "If I hadn't been in such a rush... I'm sorry."

So was she. More than he could possibly know. "Don't be," she said lightly, clenching her hands together to keep from running her fingers through the light covering of hair across his chest. "It's probably for the best."

Although she knew she was falling in love with him, she wasn't sure if he reciprocated. To her, making love involved a large amount of trust and, considering his difficulty in that area, she'd be foolish to take their relationship to a level he hadn't yet reached.

It had been blatantly obvious how much he'd wanted her. She'd read the hunger in his eyes and knew he'd seen it mirrored in her own. However, until she had an idea of where he stood with his emotions, she simply didn't want to be an outlet for him to ease a physical need. Ryan Gregory might be able to converse on nearly every subject under the sun, but he couldn't voice his own feelings.

No matter, she decided. They weren't working against

the clock, so she had plenty of time to nurture his faith in her.

"You're sure?"

"Of course. Besides, I wouldn't want to haul you into the ER and explain how you wrenched your knee. Can you imagine what the grapevine would say?"

"I'd be willing to risk it," he said.

"I'm not," she said, sitting on the edge. "Look at it this way. You only have five weeks and five days until your cast comes off."

He leaned seductively toward her. "There are ways to work around it."

"I'm sure, but I'm not going to be responsible for slowing down your recovery." And she wanted to give him time to trust her unconditionally.

"Spoilsport."

She ran a finger down his chest. "Just making sure you'll be in tip-top shape for the next opportunity."

His smile took on a feral gleam. "Count on it."

"I will." Realizing something had changed, she cocked her head. "Listen."

His brow wrinkled in concentration. "I don't hear anything."

"I know. The rain's stopped."

"I guess this means you're going home."

He sounded disappointed and she smiled. "I should."

"You don't have to leave. Spend the night."

Amy's heart said yes, but her brain said no. "With you? Here?"

"Sure. We managed last night."

She stared at him, incredulous at his nonchalant attitude. "After what just happened between us, do you honestly think we could share a bed and just sleep?"

A wry grin tugged at his mouth. "I guess not."

Unable to resist herself, she leaned over and brushed her

lips against his forehead. Touching his mouth with hers would ignite the conflagration all over again and she didn't know if she'd have the strength to resist him a second time. "I'll let myself out."

He grabbed her arm. "I'll see you tomorrow, won't I?"

"Just try and stop me."

# CHAPTER TEN

RYAN hobbled out of the exam room late on Monday afternoon and noticed how each slot along the hallway still held a chart. "How far behind are we?" he asked Dora.

"About three hours," she replied.

"That's better than I thought." Between seeing the few extra patients Amy had referred to him, discussing Jeanette Obermeyer's thyroid problem with the surgeon, playing catch-up with the people from last week and not being extremely adept with his crutches, he'd thrown off his entire schedule.

"You do realize we probably won't get finished until after seven," Dora commented.

"I know."

"Amy could handle a few extra cases if you'd like to steer some in her direction."

Although Dora sounded nonchalant, he recognized a subtle hint when he heard one. "I'll think about it."

Dora started for the nurse's room. "Don't think about it too long," she called over her shoulder. "Gorgeous summer evenings like this aren't a dime a dozen. I'd like to enjoy the few we get and so should you."

He grabbed the next chart. "I said I'd think about it."

She muttered something that sounded like "stubborn man" before she continued on her way.

Ryan pushed open the door and discovered his next case was an infant with prickly heat. After advising his mother to let him wear as few clothes as possible, change his diapers as soon as they were wet and to use a non-

158

prescription steroid cream several times a day on the affected areas, he left.

Maybe Dora was right. He hadn't seen anything this afternoon that Amy couldn't have handled. All of her referrals had been serious in nature and he couldn't fault her for any of her diagnoses.

"Dora," he yelled, trying to save himself a few steps.

She popped her head out of the nurse's room. "Yo."

"Where's Amy?" he asked.

She shrugged. "Somewhere around here, I suppose. Why?"

Not only was his good leg aching from the strain, but his arms were growing weary, too. He hated what he was about to do, but he had no choice.

"Find her," he snapped. "My office. You, too. *Now*."

Dora blinked in surprise before a faint smile and a knowing expression appeared on her face. "We'll be there in three shakes."

Moments after Ryan reached his office and sank into his chair, Amy and Dora strode in. "I thought you should know that Mrs Obermeyer's biopsy went well," he said.

The two women exchanged puzzled glances before Amy asked, "What does the surgeon think?"

"He won't be surprised if the report shows a malignancy, but until he gets the report, he's only guessing. He also commended you for noticing the nodule."

Amy glowed from his praise. "I'm glad for Jeanette's sake." She paused. "Is this why you called us in your office?"

He hesitated. His admission was harder to make than he'd thought. "I need help," he said flatly.

Amy's eyes widened. "You do?"

"Don't look so surprised," he said wryly. "You knew I would."

"Yes, but I didn't know if you'd actually acknowledge it."

"Well, I have." He addressed Dora. "Ask my patients if they would mind if Amy examined them. Considering how long a wait they've had and can still expect, I doubt if many of them will refuse."

"An excellent idea," Dora said. "Why didn't I think of it?"

Her innocent tone didn't fool Ryan, but he held back his comment and frowned. She smiled back. Actually, she beamed.

Ryan folded his arms across his chest. "You might want to get busy before I change my mind."

"I'm on it," she said cheerfully, and left.

Amy perched on the edge of his desk and swung one leg back and forth. "What brought about this change of heart?"

"I'm tired, and I have people who've been sitting here longer than necessary."

Her leg stilled. "Then you trust me with your patients?"

"I'm asking you to help me, aren't I?"

A smile gradually worked its way across her face. "I won't let you down," she said.

"I know you'll do a good job," he said. "Now, go on before I talk myself out of my brilliant idea."

She hopped off the desk. "Your wish is my command." She left with a decided bounce in her step. He only hoped he'd done the right thing.

Amy could hardly contain her excitement as she left Ryan's office. She was finally making progress. By the time Dr Feldman removed Ryan's cast, Ryan would think she was indispensable.

She stopped Dora in the hallway. "Dr Gregory looked worn out. Can you take him a cup of coffee and some of those sugar cookies Tess brought? He needs an energy boost.''

"Will do,'' she said. "And if there's any way possible for us to finish before six-thirty, I'd be forever grateful.''

"I'll try,'' Amy said.

Her first patient was a boy of eight who had several red lesions on his arms and neck. "I have no idea what Brandon got into,'' his mother reported. "At first I thought it was dry skin, but the sores are getting bigger.''

Amy took one look at the flat, circular patches, noted the scaly borders and instantly diagnosed his problem. "Do these areas itch?''

He nodded.

"I've told him not to scratch, but he doesn't listen,'' his mother said. "We tried using hydrocortisone cream in case he was allergic to something, but it hasn't helped.''

Amy pulled on a pair of latex gloves and removed a sterile scalpel and a small screw-capped bottle from the counter's top drawer. "Do you have any pets?''

"A kitty,'' Brandon answered.

"Has your kitty been sick? Lost any hair?''

Brandon's mother stared at her in amazement. "How did you know? We're treating her for ringworm.''

"Your kitty has just shared her problem with your son,'' Amy said.

"Brandon has *ringworm*?'' She sounded horrified.

"In medical terms, we call it tinea corporis because it's affecting his body. If the fungus had infected his scalp, we'd call it tinea capitas.''

"I've heard of people getting ringworm, but I never dreamed that was his problem,'' she said, clearly shocked by the idea.

Amy pulled her little stool close to the exam table and motioned for the boy to hold out one affected arm while she sat down. With his attention riveted to the scalpel in her hand, he reluctantly obeyed.

"I know this looks like I'm going to do something horrible to you," she told him, "but I'm not. All I'm going to do is scrape your skin and put the flakes in the jar. It won't hurt a bit."

He shrank away and clutched his arm close to his body. "Will it bleed?"

"No."

"And you're sure it won't hurt?"

"It will tickle more than it will hurt."

Wearing a dubious expression, he stuck out his arm.

Using enough pressure to dislodge the skin cells but not enough to cause bleeding, Amy scraped the scaly edges and dropped the flakes into the small jar. "What's your kitty's name?"

"Kitty," Brandon replied as he watched her in fascination.

Amy exchanged a humorous glance with his mother. "I should have known." Once she'd collected enough material to satisfy the lab's requirements for a potassium hydroxide prep, she took a culture swab and rubbed it vigorously over another lesion.

"OK," she said as she put away her equipment. "How did I do?"

"You were right. It didn't hurt." His wide grin exposed a missing front tooth.

"I'm sending these samples for a culture," she told his mother. "It will take several weeks to get a report because fungi grow slowly. In the meantime, I'm going to prescribe an antifungal cream. Use it until the patches clear, then continue for another two weeks."

His mother nodded. "OK."

"Bring him back if you don't see any improvement in

three or four weeks or if the lesions appear to become infected and start oozing.''

"All right.''

"I'd also recommend that you sterilize any towels, wash cloths, linens or clothes that might have come in contact with these patches," Amy advised. "You certainly don't want this to spread through your entire family.''

"Oh, heavens. I never thought of that." Brandon's mother squared her shoulders. "I'll start the laundry as soon as I get home.''

Amy stripped off her gloves and washed her hands. "And, Brandon, keep the kitty away from your face until she's better. You don't want the ringworm to spread where it will be *really* noticeable.''

"I can still hug her, can't I?" he asked, obviously worried he would be denied the pleasure.

His mother interrupted. "For what it's worth, the cat is getting better. Her hair is growing back.''

"All right," Amy said. "But be careful. You don't want to reinfect the kitty." She wasn't certain if that was possible, but she'd rather err on the side of caution.

"I will," Brandon promised.

After the two left, Amy continued to make inroads into the number of waiting patients. Occasionally, she passed Ryan in the hallway and soon the last person had been seen and sent home.

"I'm impressed with you two," Dora said. "Six-fifteen and we're done. I thought for sure we'd be here until ten o'clock tonight.''

"Come, now," Ryan said. "I wasn't *that* slow.''

Dora winked. "We'll never know, will we? Are we going to do the same thing tomorrow?''

Amy glanced at Ryan, waiting for his response. She'd wondered the same thing and mentally blessed the nurse for posing the question she hadn't drummed up enough nerve to ask.

Ryan addressed Amy. "Can you squeeze a few more patients into your schedule?"

Inside, she was shouting for joy. Outwardly, she forced herself to appear calm. "Sure. Anything to help you out."

"Then we'll follow the same routine tomorrow," he decided. "But only *if* I fall behind again."

"Of course," Amy answered. She wanted to kiss him, but restrained herself for a more private moment. Although Dora and Tess knew she was spending more of her free time with him, she wasn't ready to let her feelings become quite so obvious.

Although she arrived home later than usual, she still had time to exercise Mindy and drop by Ryan's house for a sandwich before they relaxed on his deck with a bowl of her favorite popcorn and watched the stars come out one by one.

"I appreciate what you did today," she said, stroking Mindy's head as she lay between their two lawn chairs. "I know how hard it was for you to route your patients to me."

"It was time," he said rather abruptly. Intuition told her that he didn't care to discuss it, so she let the subject drop. It would have been nice to hear him say how much he trusted her abilities, but she believed that his actions spelled out what he couldn't verbalize.

She steered the conversation in another direction. "What's the first thing you want to do when your cast comes off?"

His mouth slowly curved into a grin. He wondered what she'd say if he described what he *really* wanted to do. "I don't know. What would you suggest?"

"Dancing," she said promptly.

"I have two left feet."

"We could sign up for lessons."

He visualized the Fred Astaire and Ginger Rogers-type steps with people standing around to watch in awe as they dipped and twirled around the floor. A shudder went down his spine. "I don't think so."

"I know," she said brightly. "The high school theatre group is always asking for people to fill acting parts. We could—"

Perform in front of a crowd? "No."

"How about a swimming party? Jodie wouldn't mind if we borrowed her pool."

"Have you noticed how I'm always getting wet?"

"It has been in the upper nineties," she said. "Water events are a natural way to cool off."

"So is sitting under a shady tree."

"OK. I'll mark white-water rafting off our list."

"Good idea."

She smiled coyly. "Do you feel the same way about sun-drenched beaches?"

He chuckled. "There's an idea. Unfortunately, I won't be taking any vacations for a while. Prospective partners have to pull their weight."

"Surely Dr Hyde and the others won't mind if you're gone a few days."

"I've already had time off because of my accident."

"That's just it. It was an *accident*. Dr Hyde isn't going to hold it against you."

"He wants a return on his investment. He won't get it if I'm not practicing medicine."

"He was joking," she said, dismissing his argument. "Dr Hyde won't sacrifice his partners' health for a buck."

"Maybe not, but I'm not a fully fledged partner yet. I don't want to do anything to ruin my chances." He thought of his previous practice, and of how the man he'd worked with had rescinded his offer after Ryan had questioned the way he'd handled the case of appendicitis.

"If Dr Hyde made you an offer, he won't renege."

"Perhaps, but I want to be sure." He glanced at her. "How did we get onto the subject of my partnership? I thought we were talking about a simple celebration?"

"We were," she assured him. "Do you have *any* suggestions on how you want to proverbially kick up your heels in honor of retiring your crutches?"

"Not right now," he said. "I'm not a kick-up-your-heels kind of guy."

"Hmm," she said, tapping an index finger to her temple. "I'll simply have to think of something."

"Now, *that* sounds scary."

Amy shifted position and stretched. "It isn't. Don't worry, whatever I find to do will be fun."

"Nothing too wild," he cautioned.

She ticked off the points on her fingers. "Let me get this straight. You want intellectual slash cultural but not particularly active. Fun but not wild. It's a good thing I have five more weeks until D-day."

"You're the one who wanted to celebrate," he reminded her. "A quiet evening at home would suit me just fine."

"We're having those now. We need to do something *different*. By the way, Josh told me that Tony is doing great. He'll probably go home this week."

"What about his father? Is he still in jail?"

"Afraid so. He couldn't post bail. Shawna told me she's filing for a divorce."

"I hate to see any couple split up, but in their case I think she's made the right choice."

"And what exactly are you looking for in a wife?"

The crickets filled the momentary silence while Ryan considered his answer. "Someone who shares my interests," he said slowly. "Someone who can carry on a conversation, who likes to travel and who I can challenge to a game of chess.''

''Chess?'' Her voice sounded strained. ''I barely know the names of the pieces, much less their moves.''

''I can teach you.''

''But you don't have a chess set.''

''It's in the closet. I usually play on the Internet. So do you want to learn?'' The thought of teaching Amy the game sounded like fun. His reward for capturing each piece could easily make a single game last into the night.

A slow smile appeared. ''If you'll take dance lessons.''

He chuckled. ''You don't give up, do you?''

''Not usually.''

''So you don't care to expand your mind?''

''Hey,'' she protested. ''I like concerts and lectures and museums as much as the next person. At times, though, I simply prefer being more…lively. You should try it some time.''

''The last time I was being *lively*, as you call it, I got run over by a teenager on a scooter.''

She giggled. ''It was sort of funny. In an unusual sort of way.''

''I'm glad you're amused,'' he said dryly.

''Laughing beats crying, any day.''

And therein lay their differences, he thought. As much as he wanted to spend his hours with her, he wondered if he was setting himself up for heartbreak. He had a sneaking suspicion that she saw him as her current ''cause''—as someone she wanted to change and make over into something he wasn't.

The parallels between them and his parents were too close to be ignored. Would she, like his mother, grow frustrated, angry and then bored with him? His parents' marriage had fallen apart for that very reason, so he was a fool to think that he, under like circumstances, would fare any better.

"Can you believe this?" Pam marched down the hallway to corner Amy. "We're out of gloves. There was a snafu in the shipment and we won't get any until tomorrow. Can I borrow a few boxes?"

Amy motioned toward her nurse's room. "Check the cabinet on the left. Help yourself."

"Thanks." Pam studied her for a moment. "You're certainly chipper. As my granny would say, bright-eyed and bushy-tailed."

"Life couldn't be better," Amy answered. For the past ten days, she'd felt as if all of her dreams had come to fruition. Ryan had turned over more responsibility to her; they'd built a good working rapport, and she was certain he was falling in love with her, even if he hadn't realized it yet.

"Then Dr Gregory has finally realized what a rare and perfect gem you are?"

She grinned. "I don't know about the rare or perfect part, but I think so."

Pam clapped her on the back. "Good job. See? All you needed was a dose of patience."

"I don't think it was as much my patience as his broken ankle," she said ruefully. "Whatever the reason, though, things couldn't be better."

Pam winked. "Yeah. I heard how you've been quite a help to Dr Gregory while he's been *laid up*, so to speak."

Amy's face warmed.

"I'm happy for you, Amy," Pam said. "Although I'd love to stay and chat, I'd better run. Dr Brooks has been grumpy ever since his ex-wife has taken him to court to raise his child-support payments and I'd rather keep a low profile. I thought he'd blow a gasket when he discovered we'd run out of gloves.''

Minutes after Pam had left, Mollie came in. Her shoulders were slumped and her eyes were red. "What's wrong?" Amy asked.

Mollie sighed. "Nothing."

Amy folded her arms. "Come on. What gives?"

"Well, you know my boyfriend and I broke up last week."

Amy remembered it well. Mollie had sniffled all afternoon and used an entire box of tissues.

"Well, we'd talked about getting back together but I found out this afternoon that he's taking out *someone else* tonight."

Amy patted her shoulder. "Oh, honey, I'm sorry."

"The worst part is, the girl is one of those nerdy kids. You know, the kind who studies all the time and doesn't have a life? I just want to *die*."

"Have you talked to your mom?"

Mollie rolled her black-outlined eyes. "She doesn't understand."

"I'm sure she does," Amy told her gently. "We've all gone through this at one time or another."

Mollie sniffled and rubbed her nose with the palm of her hand. "Would you mind if I took off this afternoon?"

"You work for your mom. It's up to her to decide."

"She said it was OK with her as long as it was OK with you."

Sensing the girl wouldn't be much use to them in her current mental state, Amy agreed. "Don't sit home and mope. Call a friend. Go to a movie."

Mollie shrugged. "Maybe. See ya Monday."

Amy walked into Tess's office. "Mollie's really upset."

Tess sighed. "Don't I know it. I thought she was adjusting after they broke up a few days ago, but then this happened." She shook her head. "I predict a horrible weekend for all of us."

"Let's hope not."

Ryan came through the door. "What's with Mollie? She nearly ran over me on her way out."

Amy answered. "Boyfriend problems."

"Oh. Is that all?"

"Is that all?" Amy echoed. "Isn't it enough?"

"Well…I thought it was something serious," he said defensively.

Honestly, men could be so dense at times. "To her, it is," Amy said. "Just give her time."

"If you say so. Have you seen the prenatal reports for Melissa Horner?"

Tess handed over several sheets of paper. "Just came in today's mail."

"Thanks," he said, before he presumably returned to his office.

"So what are you doing tonight?" Tess asked her.

"Laundry and housework," Amy said promptly.

"You're not going out with Dr Gregory?" At Amy's startled glance, Tess teased her. "You don't think you could keep this news a secret for ever, could you?"

"I guess not. Besides, we didn't plan anything special because he's on call tonight."

"What about this weekend?"

"We talked about driving to Wichita to see my sister, Rachel. She's getting tickets to the Crown Uptown dinner theatre."

"Sounds like fun. What are they performing?"

"I have no idea, but I'm sure it will be good."

"Think of me at home with a sullen teenager while you're enjoying yourself."

"I will," Amy promised. Their trip to Wichita had a twofold purpose. Not only did she want to get away from

Maple Corners with Ryan, but she wanted to see if her intuition about Rachel was right or wrong. The last time she'd spoken to her sister, Rachel had sounded preoccupied and not at all like herself. She'd alluded to problems at work, but Amy suspected it was something more personal and she wanted to talk to her face to face.

She also hoped that the more time she spent with Ryan, the sooner he would see how wonderful they were together in spite of their differing personalities. The fact that they *weren't* identical was one of the things she loved about him, but she sensed that he didn't quite agree. Her dream was for him to decide that they could make a life together.

In the meantime, he was sorely testing her patience.

Ryan finished reading the newspaper and refolded it along its original creases. He hated to admit it, but he was bored with his own company. Desperate, he'd opened the gate and coaxed Mindy to sit beside him on his deck. Amy had come out once to shake out a rug and had seen her dog lying at his feet. She'd smiled and waved before she'd gone back inside.

Now it was nearly eight-thirty. He'd expected her to come over before now. How long did it take to clean a house with only one occupant? Two, if he counted Mindy.

His pager beeped. Recognizing the ER phone number on the display, he dialed it on his mobile.

"We have a possible overdose on one of your patients," the nurse informed him. "Her mother asked us to call you."

He went on instant alert. "Who is it?"

"Mollie Michaels."

"I'll be right there." He dialed Amy's phone number and got a busy signal. Walking across the yard was an option, but it would take too much time. She'd have to hear the news later. And as soon as he got through, he'd give her a hard time for not subscribing to the "call waiting" service from the local phone company.

Leaving Mindy with running rights to both yards, he drove to the hospital and conferred with Dr Jenkins, the ER physician, who was seated behind the counter.

"Mollie came in confused and highly agitated," she said. "Her friend reported that she was hallucinating, so she brought her here. We've seen the same symptoms, along with drowsiness and tachycardia."

Only one thing came to mind. "Drug abuse?"

"Both her mother and her friend say no and Mollie's pockets were clean. I went ahead and ordered a urine screen, including the usual alcohol, acetaminophen and salicylate levels. She's on $O_2$ and IV Ringer's. The ECG tech is running a strip right now. If Mollie did OD, we need to know what she took. Right now, I'm clueless."

Ryan nodded. "I'll see what I can find out." He strode into the waiting room in search of Tess.

She was seated facing the ER doors and shot to her feet as soon as she saw him. "How is she? What's wrong with her? And don't tell me what Dr Jenkins said, because I don't believe it. Mollie doesn't take drugs."

Ryan motioned for her to sit down while he did likewise. "She's showing signs of a chemical toxicity. For us to treat her properly, we need to know what the chemical is."

Tess's eyes filled with tears. "I have no idea."

Mollie's friend spoke up. "Mollie wouldn't take drugs. She just wouldn't."

"She's ingested something," he said firmly. "Either on purpose or by accident. What about aspirin or acetaminophen?"

"I have no idea," Tess said. "She's past the age where she asks me if she can take over-the-counter meds."

"Where did you go?" he asked the girl. "Could someone have slipped anything into her drink?"

"We went to McDonald's and then drove around. Just the two of us."

"Her pockets were clean. Did she have a purse with her?"

The girl looked at him as if he'd grown two heads. "Well, yeah. It's out in my car."

"Could you get it, please?"

She scampered outside. "Do you think you'll find something?" Tess asked.

"It would make our job easier if I did," he said.

A few minutes later, the teen returned with Mollie's small gray shoulder-bag. She handed it to him. "Isn't this like an invasion of privacy?"

"We're trying to save her life, not read her diary." He rummaged through until his fingers brushed against a vial.

He pulled it out. The distinctive pharmaceutical bottle was labeled as containing a tricyclic antidepressant. It also had Mollie's name printed in bold letters.

"I didn't know Mollie took an antidepressant," he said, showing Tess the vial.

"I didn't either." Tess looked as shocked as he felt. "I haven't taken her to a doctor for depression, so where did she get it? Who gave it to her?"

The answers were on the label and his heart flip-flopped as he read the name. It didn't seem possible, but it was there in black and white. "Amy."

"Amy? *Our* Amy?"

Ryan nodded, trying to think of a reason for the high dose and failing.

"I don't believe it," Tess said flatly. "There must be some mistake. Amy wouldn't do such a thing without telling me."

"She did," he said flatly. Holding the bottle in his hand, he maneuvered himself back through the ER doors and handed Dr Jenkins the vial. "Here's your problem."

She read the label. "It's rather a strong dose for a kid her size, isn't it?" Without waiting for his reply, she turned to the nurses hovering nearby. "We need to set up for gastric lavage and multiple-dose activated charcoal. Call the lab and ask them to add a screen for TCA to the blood sample they've already drawn. Let's get moving."

While the staff scattered to implement her orders, Ryan talked to Tess and telephoned Amy. This time, he got through to her answering machine. He left a message, then waited in ER for Mollie to receive her first dose of charcoal.

Thirty minutes later, Amy burst through the doors. "Tess said Mollie OD'd on an antidepressant? How did that happen?"

Ryan pulled her into a small med. room for privacy. "You tell me," he said grimly.

Amy frowned. "Why would I know anything about it?"

"Because you prescribed it for her."

"I did no such thing."

"Deny it all you want," he said. "But your name is right here in black and white." He showed her the vial.

She slowly sank onto a nearby chair. "I never prescribed this. Period. You have to believe me."

He leaned closer. "Then how do you explain it?"

"I can't."

He pressed on. "She was upset and you—"

"I *talked* to her," she insisted. "I didn't give her a prescription or imply she needed medication."

"According to the date, she's had this for some time," he pointed out. "Why did you choose this particular drug when there are others that don't carry the side effects? More important, what were you thinking to write it for this high a dose?"

She met his gaze without wavering. "You don't believe I'm telling the truth, do you?"

He waved the bottle. "The evidence speaks for itself."

Amy came to her feet, her eyes glistening. "Your evidence is wrong." With that, she strode out of the room.

# CHAPTER ELEVEN

AMY stepped into Mollie's cubicle and found Tess standing next to her bed, holding her hand. "I didn't prescribe the medication," she said flatly.

"When Dr Gregory told me, I couldn't believe it," Tess admitted. "I still can't. But how would she have gotten the pills without a script, and why is your name listed as the one who ordered it?"

Amy had one patient who was taking an antidepressant, and she recalled Mollie's interest in the drug. Her idea was a long shot, but until she talked to Mollie she was only guessing.

"I'm not sure," she said.

"Does Dr Gregory have any theories?"

"He has one," Amy said bitterly. "He thinks I arranged for her to have the pills."

"But if you explained that you didn't—"

"He didn't believe me."

Amazement appeared on Tess's face. "As close as you two have been, how could he not?" she asked.

Amy shrugged. "It's easy. He's been waiting for me to make a mistake."

"He should know better," she declared.

Amy pretended that this incident didn't bother her. "He should, but he doesn't."

The lines on Tess's face deepened and she lowered her voice. "As much as I hate to admit this or even think about it, Mollie may have done something she shouldn't have. She has access to a lot of things, including prescription pads. Do you suppose…?"

"Let's not get wrought up until we hear Mollie's story."

Tess bit her lip. "You're right. We'll deal with the situation then."

Mollie stirred. Her eyelids fluttered and she raised her arm to touch her forehead. "Mom?" she asked sleepily.

Tess bent down. "Yes, hon. I'm here."

Mollie started to cry. "I don't feel so good."

"I know." Tears glistened in Tess's eyes.

"It was an accident. I swear."

"Just relax," Tess told her, stroking the hair out of Mollie's face. "We'll talk later."

Relieved by Mollie's response and her obvious first steps on the road to recovery, Amy suddenly felt exhausted. "I'm going now," she murmured to Tess. "If you need me, call."

"Thanks for coming," Tess answered.

Amy left the cubicle and saw Ryan sitting behind the nurse's counter. Aware of attracting his attention, she squared her shoulders, tossed him a glance capable of melting his aluminum crutches and strode on past. She didn't know what hurt worse—his distrust or the fact that he let her leave without a word.

The pain of his rejection went so deep she was numb from the shock. Everything they'd shared had become infinitely precious to her, but for him to desert her at a moment's notice made her feel as if he'd only been using her to amuse himself.

At least she hadn't told him that she loved him. It would be hard enough to see him at the clinic without her impetuous declaration hanging between them. Her pride wouldn't have stood the strain.

At home, she didn't bother with lights except for one small lamp in the living room, preferring the darkness because it completely matched her gloomy spirits. Normally, Mindy was waiting on the patio, her nose pressed to the glass in anticipation of being allowed inside. Tonight, however, she wasn't.

Amy tugged on the door, expecting the spaniel to streak through the opening. When Mindy still didn't appear, Amy flicked on the outdoor light. Her yard was empty, but the gate between hers and Ryan's stood ajar.

There, in the shadows covering Ryan's patio, sat Mindy, looking quite content.

"Traitor," Amy mumbled under her breath before she called the spaniel's name.

Mindy stretched, clearly happy to stay where she was. Amy, however, wasn't. She marched to the gate and yelled a second time in a tone she used only after Mindy had committed a major offense. As the dog slunk through the opening, tail between her legs, Amy slammed the gate closed. She would have loved to have fixed a padlock in place as a clear "unwelcome" sign to her neighbor, but she didn't have one.

She went inside and stuffed a change of clothes in an overnight bag. She didn't want to drive to Wichita, but the best way to get over her heartache was to focus on someone else. Rachel would be that person. The advice she'd given Mollie had been sound and she intended to follow it herself.

Tears burned at the back of her eyes, but she refused to let them fall. She wasn't going to waste her time crying over a man who didn't trust her, who couldn't give her the benefit of the doubt and who was quick to believe the worst.

Even as she cited each reason, the moisture spilled out of her eyes and down her cheeks. She mourned all her losses tonight, and they were many.

The clinic simply wouldn't be the same. Their working relationship had been damaged beyond repair. Her life would be worse than it had been when Ryan had first arrived. She wouldn't be allowed to prescribe an aspirin without his approval.

Anger began to build. He should have believed her, taken her at her word. Tess did.

*Tess doesn't carry the baggage that he does.*

A poor excuse, she told the little voice in her head. Even in the presence of damning evidence, her friend had remained open-minded.

Maybe she should have explained her theory, but she hadn't had one at the time. She could offer it now, but Ryan wouldn't pay attention. She would sound as if she were shifting the blame to save herself and she refused to beg him to believe her.

Sure, she'd made mistakes, but she'd always owned up to them. If he was waiting for her to admit her culpability in Mollie's case, he'd wait a long time. She simply wasn't guilty.

In that instant she knew what she had to do. She'd talk to Dr Hyde and either request a transfer or hand in her resignation. She didn't have the patience to regain the ground she'd lost tonight through no fault of her own. Even if she did, there wouldn't be enough years in her lifetime to accomplish that feat.

Mollie's incident had not only destroyed their professional camaraderie, it had completely severed their personal relationship. Without a foundation of trust, love would never grow. It was time to cut her losses and relegate Ryan Gregory to the past.

Walking away had never been a problem for her. She'd been beaten down before, but she'd always bounced back and regained her ability to enjoy life. This time, though, she didn't expect to make such a rapid recovery. Ryan had meant too much to her to pretend otherwise. It would be a long time before her heart mended, if ever.

She might have grown tired of starting over but, come Monday morning, she would.

"Tell me about the pills," Ryan said to Mollie the next morning. Although she was still groggy, most of her other adverse reactions had either improved or disappeared completely. He, on the other hand, had spent a sleepless night trying to arrive at an explanation for Amy's name being on a prescription she supposedly hadn't written. He wanted to believe Amy but, with the evidence in hand, what choice did he have?

The flash of vulnerability in her eyes and in her stance before she'd squared her shoulders and sailed out of the ER had made him wonder if this situation might not be as clear-cut as he'd originally assumed. Doubt had raised its head, which was why he'd come to see Mollie first thing this morning.

Mollie looked away. "Do I have to?"

"Yes, you do," he said. "Do you know what they're for?"

She nodded. "Depression."

"And are you depressed?" he asked gently.

"Sometimes."

"How many did you take?"

"One more than the bottle said." She rubbed her nose with the back of her hand. "I've never taken the pills before, but Amy said they were for people who were so overwhelmed by their problems that they couldn't function. Since I was *really* down, with my boyfriend dumping me, I thought it would help."

He played his hunch. "And Amy OK'd this?"

Not meeting his gaze, she shook her head.

"Yet she wrote the prescription," he pressed, determined to get to the bottom of the mystery.

"She did," Mollie said in a small voice, "but…"

"But what?" he coaxed.

"But she wrote it for someone else," she blurted. Once she'd admitted that much, it was as if she couldn't hold the rest of the story back. "A lady was coming in one afternoon to pick up this script. I didn't recognize the drug, so Amy explained what it was used for. I thought it would be cool to be able to pop a pill whenever I felt depressed. So I covered up the real patient's name and photocopied the page. The copy looked better than the original."

"And you took it to the pharmacy."

"Yeah. I'm in trouble, aren't I?"

He drew a deep breath. The teenager had answered his questions and vindicated Amy, but now he knew how a condemned man felt. She would never forgive him.

"I'm afraid so," he told Mollie. "What you did was illegal, not to mention dangerous. I hope you learned your lesson about taking medicine that's not meant for you."

Mollie's eyes widened. "I have. I promise not to do it again."

"Trust is a fragile thing," he said. "Once it's lost, it's hard to regain." Mentally, he winced as his speech hit home.

"I know but, honestly, I will never, ever do anything like this again for as long as I live."

He rose and slipped his crutches under his arms. "Good, because if you do, I'm going to turn you over my knee, no matter how big you are."

Mollie's fearful expression eased. "Deal."

Ryan left the hospital, his thoughts racing. He should have believed Amy had been telling the truth. Why else would she have maintained her innocence, knowing how easily he could disprove her claim—talking to the pharmacy staff, for instance. Yet, even with the potential of records proving her wrong, she'd still denied her involvement. Now he couldn't shake the guilt that ruthlessly plagued him. He should have accepted Amy's word and discussed the situation rationally. Instead, he'd acted as judge and jury in one fell swoop.

To think he'd looked upon Amy's impulsive streak with disdain. From the way he jumped to conclusions, he clearly had a measure of the same shortcoming.

He sauntered across the doctor's parking lot to his car, already feeling the heat scorch the top of his head. Of course, it wasn't nearly as uncomfortable as being on the receiving end of Amy's hostility. He shouldn't have been waiting for—no, *expecting*—Amy to shortchange her patients, especially after he'd seen her in action.

He'd done her a total injustice and deserved every mental dagger she'd thrown in his direction.

Eager to clear the air, he speeded toward Amy's house, although he didn't expect her to welcome him with open arms. An apology was in order, along with whatever penance was necessary to make up for his error. All he could do was beg for a second chance.

From the way she'd glared at him in the ER, he didn't hold out much hope for her mercy, but he had to try. He wanted their relationship restored to its pre-Mollie days, although as angry as she'd been it could easily take a long time for that to happen. Whatever her faults, they paled in comparison to a lifetime spent without her.

His grandfather had been right. *This* was love, plain and simple.

An air of emptiness surrounded Amy's property. He remembered their plans to go to Wichita, so he assumed she hadn't cancelled them. Disheartened at not being able to settle matters then and there, he resigned himself to wait until she returned.

As he walked through his house, his crutches creaking in the silence, his former haven now seemed as silent as a tomb. The thought of Amy not curling up on his sofa or raiding his cupboards for popcorn pained him. Home didn't seem like home without her.

Most likely, she'd request a transfer back to Dr Jackson, but he didn't intend to let that happen. He didn't want her working for anyone else.

He may have handled a lot of things poorly, but he desperately wanted to undo the damage he'd caused. He'd hurt her, and now he intended to do what he could to heal those hurts.

It was his own flaw that made him wary of others, his parents and colleagues included. Amy had tried to tell him to judge everyone on their own merits, but he hadn't and now he was paying the price for his stubbornness. He'd thought to protect himself, to save himself grief by being cautious, but this time his wariness had resulted in his own heartache. However, as he'd told her before, he learned from his mistakes and this was one mistake he would not repeat.

Early on Monday morning, Amy sat in Dr Hyde's office with her hands folded on her lap. "I'd like a transfer," she said calmly.

He appeared thoughtful as he steepled his fingers and pressed them to his mouth. "Why?"

"Dr Gregory's and my personalities don't mesh. We disagree on too many things."

"I see. Maybe you haven't allowed enough time to iron out all the kinks…"

"We've had plenty of time," she said. "I'm simply not able to work with him any longer."

He frowned. "That's funny. Ryan didn't give the same impression when I spoke with him yesterday."

The news caught her by surprise, but she quickly recovered. "I'm sorry, but I think it best if I work elsewhere."

"Hmm," he said, wearing his pensive expression once

again. "I assume this has something to do with the events of this past weekend?"

She hesitated. Explaining the situation out loud somehow made it seem all the more real and all the more painful. Swallowing hard, she said, "Dr Gregory doesn't trust me."

"Are you certain?"

"There's no question."

"Ryan's taken some hard knocks. Maybe you're not seeing distrust, *per se*, but an overdeveloped sense of responsibility. Why, he even tried to take the blame for what happened."

Amy was stunned. "Why would he do that?"

Dr Hyde shrugged. "Because both you and Mollie work for him. He also asked if this incident would affect our partnership. Naturally, I reassured him on that score. It's not his fault young Mollie acted foolishly."

"No, it's not," she said slowly, remembering how his previous partner had shortchanged him. Ryan had certainly run into more than his share of scoundrels. Would she have reacted in the same way if those incidents had happened to her?

No matter, she thought firmly. He shouldn't assume those experiences were the norm because they weren't. If he'd only open his eyes, he'd see it was true.

Dr Hyde continued. "What impressed me the most about him is that he's extremely thorough. I'm sure you'd say the same."

She couldn't argue his point. Ryan didn't run his office like an assembly line—he gave each patient his undivided attention.

He rose. "You might consider these things before you make any decision. However, if you truly feel you can't work with Dr Gregory and if he agrees to let you go, I'll see what I can do. Otherwise…"

"He'll agree." He'd probably help her clean out her desk

and figure out a way to personally haul her belongings to her new location.

She ambled back to her area of the building. Crossing the hallway leading from her wing to Dr Hyde's, she saw Ryan approaching at a clip much too fast for a man on crutches. Determination was carved on his features, but as soon as he saw her his expression changed. He slowed down and a flash of resignation appeared before it was replaced by his usual calm.

"Good morning, Amy," he said evenly. "Did you have a nice weekend?"

"I've had more enjoyable ones." Rachel's misery had matched her own and Amy had returned to Maple Corners as emotionally drained as when she'd left. A quick glance showed he hadn't fared much better. Lines bracketed his mouth and shadows seemed to fill his eyes.

"Have you seen Tess? Or Mollie?" he asked.

"I called them last night."

"Then you know what happened."

"Yes." She drew a deep breath and forced herself to proceed. "Before you say anything else, I should tell you I've spoken with Dr Hyde."

"I assumed you would." He hesitated for the space of a breath. "It may not make any difference to you now, but I'd really like to talk."

She had little to say, but it was best relayed in private. "How about the courtyard?"

"Fine."

The courtyard was a small area created when a second wing had been added perpendicular to the main building. Weather permitting, staff sometimes ate their lunches there while those who smoked came regularly to satisfy their habit. At this time of day, it was empty.

She waited for him to choose one of the wrought-iron chairs before she sat in the one opposite. Seeing no point in prolonging the inevitable, she cut right to the chase. "Dr Hyde's agreed to transfer me to another physician if you don't object."

He pursed his lips in a tight frown. "I *do* object. Whole-heartedly."

Bewildered, Amy stared at him. "How can you refuse? You don't trust me. Why would you want me around?"

"I love you, Amy."

She'd waited for so long to hear him say those words, but it was too late. A lump formed in her throat and she blinked rapidly to lessen the burning sensation in her eyes. She shook her head and waved her hands as if her motion would negate his comment. "No, you don't. You can't love me if you don't trust me. One builds upon the other."

"I agree. I was a fool."

She hooted in derision. "You got that right."

"I didn't look past the obvious. My intuition said that you couldn't have made such a mistake, but I let the evidence persuade me otherwise. I should have given you the benefit of the doubt and talked to Mollie before I accused you of wrongdoing. I screwed up."

Obviously he felt badly about what he'd done, but she wasn't ready to let him off the hook so easily. "Tell me something I don't know."

"I love you, Amy."

She felt her resolve wavering at his repeated statement, but she refused to give in. "You told me once that trust was earned. I'm sorry, but I find your declaration extremely hard to swallow."

"I know. Which is why I intend to prove how sincere I am."

She jumped to her feet, unable to sit still. "What brought on the change of heart?"

"I've always tried to save myself from being disappointed," he said slowly. "But my greatest disappointment will be if I let you slip through my fingers. I do trust you, Amy. My heart knew it all along, but my head was more difficult to convince.''

"Do you really believe what you're saying?" If he was only telling her what he thought she wanted to hear...

"Absolutely. If you can hang on to your inherent faith in people even after your experience with the Mullens, then I want to learn how, too. I'm asking you to be patient enough to teach me.''

She slowly shook her head. "I don't know if that's possible. We're so different that I'm not sure if—''

"We can make it work," he insisted. "Of course, we don't share all the same interests, but I'm willing to compromise, if you are.''

His matter-of-fact tone started to thaw the frozen region around her heart. "You are?''

His gaze didn't waver as he slowly nodded.

She was overwhelmed by the unexpected twists to this conversation. "I don't know what to say.''

"How about, 'I forgive you for being an idiot'? Or, 'I want to forget the transfer'?''

Amy wanted to repeat those phrases, but she had one crucial point to iron out. "What about the next time something happens? Will you judge first and ask questions later?''

"I sincerely hope not," he said fervently. "But if I should happen to forget, I'm counting on you to remind me.''

Tears came to her eyes. "Oh, Ryan," she said, choking on her words.

Ryan rose and hobbled to her side on one crutch before he gathered her close with his free arm. "Then you'll give me a second chance?''

She didn't have to think twice. "Yeah. So don't blow it.''

"No way." He wiped off the moisture on her face with his fingers. "In case you're interested, I've decided what I want to do after Feldman springs me from my cast."

Still in the circle of his embrace, she leaned back to stare into his eyes. "What intellectual, cultural, non-wild activity did you think of?"

He grinned. "To dance at our wedding."

**Modern Romance**™
...seduction and
passion guaranteed

**Tender Romance**™
...love affairs that
last a lifetime

**Sensual Romance**™
...sassy, sexy and
seductive

*Blaze*
...sultry days and
steamy nights

**Medical Romance**™
...medical drama on
the pulse

**Historical Romance**™
...rich, vivid and
passionate

*29 new titles every month.*

*With all kinds of Romance for
every kind of mood...*

MILLS & BOON®

*Makes any time special*™

MAT4

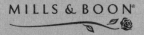

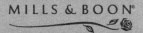

## 4 Books
### and a surprise gift!

We would like to take this opportunity to thank you for reading this Mills & Boon® book by offering you the chance to take FOUR more specially selected titles from the Medical Romance™ series absolutely FREE! We're also making this offer to introduce you to the benefits of the Reader Service™—

- ★ FREE home delivery
- ★ FREE gifts and competitions
- ★ FREE monthly Newsletter
- ★ Books available before they're in the shops
- ★ Exclusive Reader Service discounts

Accepting these FREE books and gift places you under no obligation to buy; you may cancel at any time, even after receiving your free shipment. Simply complete your details below and return the entire page to the address below. *You don't even need a stamp!*

**YES!** Please send me 4 free Medical Romance books and a surprise gift. I understand that unless you hear from me, I will receive 6 superb new titles every month for just £2.49 each, postage and packing free. I am under no obligation to purchase any books and may cancel my subscription at any time. The free books and gift will be mine to keep in any case.

M1ZEB

Ms/Mrs/Miss/Mr ...................................................Initials................................................
BLOCK CAPITALS PLEASE

Surname.........................................................................................................................

Address.........................................................................................................................

.....................................................................................................................................

..........................................................Postcode ...................................

**Send this whole page to:**
**UK: The Reader Service, FREEPOST CN81, Croydon, CR9 3WZ**
**EIRE: The Reader Service, PO Box 4546, Kilcock, County Kildare (stamp required)**